Don't Let Go

Skye Warren

PRAISE FOR DON'T LET GO

"Perfectly dark, gritty, emotionally, fulfilling, amount in each word till the end."

—Amber's Reading Room

"My mind is completely blown! Who knew I could feel this way about Carlos? I love this author even more for what she was able to accomplish."

—Sweet Spot Book Blog

"Skye Warren, I hope you can hear me loud and clear when I say: "BRAVO!" Thanks for your wonderful dark erotica series, I'll never forget the whole twisted, thrilling and intense story and its amazing characters."

—Darkest Sins

"Don't Let Go by Skye Warren has blown me away. Skye's ability to make me feel like I am part of this dramatic, dark, and twisted story is so fucking fantastic I can only sit here and beg for more."

—Fictional Candy

"It doesn't happen often, but this book turned me inside out. If you're a fan of Criminal Minds, you might enjoy this, dark erotic twist and all."

—Ms Romantic Reads

"Don't Let Go is a riveting dark erotic story that takes the reader on one hell of a thrilling and emotional roller coaster ride. Author Skye Warren weaves a complex, deep, and haunting tale that has a raw and gritty mixture of violence and moving tenderness."

—Jersey Girl Sizzling Book Reviews

"He who fights with monsters should be careful that he himself does not become a monster. And if you gaze long into an abyss, the abyss also gazes into you."

—Friedrich Nietzsche

AUTHOR'S FOREWORD

Dear Reader,

I must warn you that this is a disturbing tale, one that starts dark and gets darker. If you are looking for a straight-laced BDSM book, this is not for you. It's intended as a fantasy for those who are as fascinated by erotic pain and consent as I am. The only balm I can offer is that I'm a romantic at heart, and I think that surfaces by the very end.

Yours,
Skye Warren

CHAPTER ONE

THERE WERE LIES people told you. Like when the case worker said, *You're going to love your new home, Samantha.*

Then there are lies you tell other people. *My father passed away.* That was what I told people, even though he'd just turned fifty-two in a supermax prison. It was easier that way. Lies smoothed the way so we could go on pretending. They were the lube of life, and we all got a little messy in the process.

But the darkest lies were the ones you told yourself. They lurked in the shadows of your subconscious, undermining you and twisting your perceptions. They hid the answers in plain sight, right when you needed them most.

Spread out on my desk were piles of surveillance photos and notes taken over the past twelve months. I found it impossible to imagine that countless field workers and researchers had managed to miss his completely. Which meant this muddled collection of reports contained the information we needed. Hiding in plain sight.

Every image, from airport security cameras to public

transportation cams to satellite imagery, showed a man with his head bent, facing down or away. As if he knew exactly where the cameras were, eluding us once again. The man looking the other direction, he could have been anyone. He probably *was* anyone, considering the pattern of times and locations didn't add up. Carlos Laguardia wasn't in a Chicago eatery known for mob connections one day, and then a Paris subway the next, and then a Florida University after that. We were grasping at straws—carefully planted straws designed to misdirect.

Only one image was different. A grainy black-and-white photograph showed a man standing still with people milling about him. Blurs brushing past a dangerous criminal. A monster. They'd run screaming if they knew all the things he'd done. I had chills just reading about it in this air-conditioned cubicle at the highly-secure FBI office.

Money laundering. Extortion. Murder. If there was a law against it, he'd done it. A wave of old pain washed over me. Men like that didn't care who they hurt, whether it was the victims of their crimes or collateral damage.

I had been collateral damage once. Twelve years ago, I'd huddled under the coffee table when my father came home late, hands crusted with blood. I should have been grateful he hadn't ever touched me, raped me, killed me. He did that to other little girls. And boys—he was an equal opportunity creep.

Until he finally made a mistake. A boy from my street had disappeared, and even at ten years old, I knew what it meant. I still remembered the heat of that August day and the cold bite of the chair beneath my legs. Static from the plastic seat zapped my skin while I waited in the police station. Horror and pity flickered over the policeman's face as I told him my story.

I learned an important lesson then: criminals always make a mistake. *Always.*

If I could figure out Laguardia's mistake, I'd have him. If I could find the little man with blue pants and a red striped shirt in this real life *Where's Waldo*, he'd be mine. Unfortunately, the heavy stack of papers on my desk wasn't talking.

This was the only image where he looked at the camera, but the resolution was too low for facial recognition software. I got the impression of patrician features—a broad forehead, a strong nose. Dark, curly hair peeked from beneath a thick skullcap. A bulky jacket obscured what looked to be a large frame of a man. Tall, compared to the people walking around him. Well, we'd always known he'd be physically fit and capable of fighting. But beneath his brawn was a mastermind who had run a global organization and eluded hundreds of trained law enforcement officers.

Not for much longer, though. The director had held an all-hands meeting last week.

"Laguardia has made a mockery of this organization," he'd said, and at the back of the room, I'd silently agreed.

"Our ideals," he'd continued, practically frothing at the mouth. "Our effectiveness. Even our dignity. A single man has turned us into a joke. That ends now. The time to get a gold star for effort has passed. It's not good enough to look for him. You're going to damn well find him. Use all the goddamn resources you need. I will find a way to get funding and support from legal, but *you* are the agents. You've got your eyes on the ground. It's up to *you* to bring him in."

That little speech had flashed me back over a decade, when I'd had my eyes on the ground. When I'd been the only one at the right time and place to capture a criminal, even if it had been my own father. Yes, I understood. Yes, I was on board, ready to catch him. Of course, as a junior agent, that would mostly involve getting coffee and making copies, but hey, that would be my contribution to bringing him down.

A soft knock came from the cubicle next to me. I peeked my head over the short beige walls.

Lance, my friend and fellow junior agent, held up a cup of baby carrots. "Want one?"

"Thanks." I grabbed one and sat back down, munching.

We had started at the Houston branch of the FBI at the same time and bonded over the completely uninteresting work we were given. Instead of glass-walled offices, we had small stubby cubicles shoved into the corner. Instead of field assignments and fancy gadgets, we did grunt work and replaced toner in the printer.

"What are you working on?" Lance said from his side.

"Looking at this case file."

A snort. He knew which one I meant. "Did you find his secret hideout yet?"

"Oh yeah," I joked airily. "I think I've got this case wrapped up tight. He should be in custody within the hour."

"I'm sure Brody will be over to thank you personally for your service."

"And offer me a raise," I added.

Our boss and regional manager, Brody, barely even knew I was alive, except when he needed coffee.

Lance's response was cut off by a commotion in the hallway. I peeked over the wall to see a wave of suits led by Brody rounding the corner, heading in my direction. Plopping back on my seat, I swiveled to face my desk and pretended to work. I actually *had* been working, in a sense, but not on the budget reports I'd been assigned. I gathered the photographs into an unruly stack and stuffed them into my desk, turning my attention to the spreadsheet blinking empty on my monitor.

Instead of quickly rushing past, as expected, the thud of footsteps slowed.

Brody peered over the ledge. "Meet us in the conference room, Ms. Holmes."

Then he was gone, and I was hyperventilating. Me? Now? The suits continued past, toward the tall-ceilinged conference room. I stared at the blank cells in the spreadsheet, heart pounding. They'd never asked me in to one of their powwows before. And everyone looked so stern—almost angry. What would they say to me? I could only imagine the worst: *you're fired. You screwed up. You don't belong here.* Unlikely, but try telling that to my racing heart.

Lance hissed at me through the cubicle wall. "What are you doing, Samantha? Go!"

"Why do they want me there?" I whispered back, stalling.

"I don't know. Maybe to take notes?"

"Oh." Relief swept through me. Immediately followed by embarrassment. "Good idea. Probably that."

Why had I freaked out over a simple conference? They wanted a secretary, for crying out loud. What was wrong with me?

Transitive guilt, the psychology textbook would say.

A tendency to assume guilt for wrongs I hadn't committed due to childhood trauma. In other words, I felt so freaking bad for what my father had done that it spilled over into my adult life.

I could self-diagnose like a pro after specializing in Criminal Behavior at Quantico. We applied a lot of psychological buzzwords to deviant behavior. But the most interesting part had been the total lack of blame present in those classes.

Maybe that was why criminal behavior studies appealed to me. We analyzed them like rats in a maze, trying to figure out what made them tick. No one blamed a rat for eating the cheese at the end. No one blamed him for wanting to escape.

The FBI knew about my dad, of course, and the part I'd played in his capture. That was fine. Plenty of agents got started because we'd seen the effects of criminal activity firsthand. They had just required that a psychologist sign off on me. That had been a cakewalk, after taking all the required classes on behavioral psychology.

What do you remember? she'd asked, again and again. Psychologists were such voyeurs. They got off on true-life confessions, and then expected us to trust them. Not likely.

Grabbing a steno pad and a pen, I hustled down the hallway where a few of the suits were heading in a different direction. A smaller meeting then. When I slipped through the heavy door, I found only two men inside.

Brody sat at the head of the cherry wood conference table, but without the full audience I was used to from the staff meetings. The other man stood at the window, turned away. I couldn't see him very well, but the gray peppered through his dark blond hair gave me a clue to his age. He kept himself fit, his body lean and exuding virility. And my last observation as a budding detective: he had power. Power enough not to wait on Brody attentively. No, he continued to gaze out the window, pensive.

"Are you going to sit down, Ms. Holmes?" Brody asked.

I'd been staring at the stranger. And caught by my boss.

A flush crept up my neck. "Yes, sir."

I slid into a seat at the opposite end of the table, pad flat and pen poised to write. Except Brody was looking at me, as if waiting for me to talk. It felt vaguely like a nightmare, walking into class and realizing I'd completely forgotten about the assignment that was due. I wished I hadn't worn this pale pink blouse I'd fallen in love with at an artisan fair. Even if it was covered by yards of stiff suiting to guard against any idea that I favored form over function.

Self-consciously, I tugged at the drop pearls hanging from my earlobes, wishing I'd skipped those too. I wanted to wash myself in professional bleach so they'd know I belonged at the table. I looked down, letting my hair brush across my face—hiding, wondering. What the hell did Brody want me to say?

Brody leaned forward, a predatory glint in his eyes. "Agent Holmes, I'm sure you know why we're here."

The only thing I was sure about was that my palms were sweating. The pen was slippery in my hand. "Sir?"

"Laguardia," he said impatiently. "The most wanted man in the United States? Surely you've heard of him."

"Yes, sir. Of course."

Shit. His stare was intimidating. It made me want to confess crimes I hadn't even committed yet. *Yet?* Where had that thought come from? I didn't even have a speeding ticket. I would never be a criminal. I would *never* be like my father. But secretly, fearfully, I'd always wondered if that was just a lie I told myself.

Brody tossed a manila folder onto the table, and a small stack of papers fanned out in front of me. "In the past year, twelve major players near Laguardia have been killed. Some of them were loyal partners. Others were competitors. In-fighting within the organization. Power struggles. They're killing each other off."

Since he seemed to be waiting for a response, I said, "Well...that's convenient for us."

A soft sound came from the man at the window, like a snort of amusement. Brody's eyes raised like I'd said something inappropriate, and I supposed I had. Only, I suspected he wasn't annoyed they were dying. Instead, he preferred we were the ones doing the killing. Or capturing.

"This is our best chance to bring them down," Brody said. "We move hard and fast. While they're licking their wounds, too busy to pay attention to what we're doing." He jerked his head toward the other man. "So I've brought in Ian Hennessey."

The man at the window inclined his head in what I assumed was a greeting or acknowledgment. But he didn't face us, even then, leaving me to make a non-committal sound in my throat. What did any of this have to do with me? Maybe Ian Hennessey—his name spoken with a certain weight—was so important he warranted his own personal coffee-fetcher. Who would be me.

When Hennessey continued to stand there, Brody

cleared his throat. "Ian is one of our best agents. He's closed a hell of a lot of cases. The Di Mariano family. And the Mencia? Maybe you've heard of it. Big jewel heist in Manhattan. A lot of high-profile cases, and now he's going to give this one a try."

"I'm not going to try," Hennessy said quietly. "I'm going to close the case."

A shiver ran down my spine at the certainty in his voice. The ferocity.

My third foster mother had a thing for the stage. Plays would come on the public programming channel, and she would watch them late at night in between requests for donations. I would huddle in the hallway in my pajamas, watching with her. To this day I wasn't sure if she figured out I was there or if she cared.

I didn't know why those plays had caught my interest, when other kids my age were into boy bands and Nickelodeon. But there was something beautiful about the music and the drama, something pure. Even when they'd dealt with cold subjects like prostitution and death, it had all seemed far more elevated than the real-life version of *Cops* my childhood had been.

Just now, with Hennessey so focused, I was reminded of *Les Miserables*. Police Inspector Javert had been bent on capturing a man who had been a thief in his former life. He became obsessed with it. Except the police inspector wasn't the hero of the story. The criminal was.

Brody cleared his throat and turned to me. "So what do you think?"

"Oh. Me?" My mind raced, trying to figure out the question. What did I think of *what*? Hennessey closing the case? "It's good. I mean, I think he will. Close the case."

"Good. And you," Brody said, his gaze clashing with mine, "are going to be his partner."

"What?" The question left my lips at the exact same time as Hennessey's. We both stared at Brody, me in confusion and Hennessy in irritation. I could guess why Hennessey was mad, the big-shot getting stuck with the rookie. The cause of my own annoyance was a little murkier.

I had been working here six months. HR had contacted me just last week with some forms I'd neglected to fill out on hiring. *NEW* was practically stamped on my forehead, but Brody was assigning me to a high-profile case? Even Lance had gotten here a month before me. It sounded fishy as hell, like some sort of equal opportunity mandate, putting a woman—*any woman*—in the field to cover their asses. I didn't want a pity assignment, even if it was my only chance.

Brody shrugged, unfazed. "Until such time as Carlos is apprehended or terminated, you two are going to be partners."

"Whose decision was this?" Hennessey asked tightly.

"Mine." Brody's gaze sharpened. "And the director's. You're free to take this over my head, but I think we both know you won't."

Hennessey swung away, staring out the window,

radiating displeasure. He wasn't sightseeing now. He was pissed. "Does she even know what happened to the last guy?"

And now I had *that* to worry about. What the hell had happened to the last guy? And the last guy of what?

"I don't see what that has to do with anything," Brody said with equanimity.

Hennessey laughed. It wasn't a nice laugh.

A shiver ran through me.

"I'll leave you two to get acquainted," Brody said, as if this were some sort of date.

In a way, it was. The arranged marriage of law enforcement partnerships. Brody shot Hennessey a glance I couldn't quite dissect before standing. Envy, maybe. As a supervisor, he could only assign the cases, not work them. And something else…a hint of concern. Concern for who, though? *Does she even know what happened to the last guy?* Shit.

Brody paused on his way out, speaking low enough for my ears only. "If you want out, tell me now. I'll speak to the director."

Gratitude pierced my growing worry. The biggest opportunity of my career, of *any* career with the Bureau, and here he was giving me a choice. I wouldn't let him down. I wouldn't let myself down. "No, sir. Happy to be here."

He nodded, granting me a rare look of approval. "Be careful." He glanced back at Hennessy. "And watch out for him, will you? He doesn't realize he's getting old."

I suppressed the laugh that wanted to escape and managed a quick nod. Clearly there was some competitiveness between them. That was common enough around here. And I could see why he felt threatened by this man. Anyone would.

Hennessy cut a striking form against the window's glow, but the silver streaking his honey-brown hair at his temples proved he was older than me. Much older, in both years and experience. Despite the obvious differences between my new partner and me, it felt good to be part of the club. A sense of contentment and happiness swelled inside me. However it had come about, this gig would lift me out of the professional gutter in a way that coffee runs and paper filing had never done.

The door closed me in with an audible click. My walk across the carpet, however, didn't make a sound. Years of rigorous training, both inside the academy and out, had left me as agile as any practiced field agent. Still, I felt sure he tracked my every movement, effortlessly, with the kind of awareness born of experience. How long had he been an agent? Ten years, twenty? Criminals had shot at him, tried to blow him up, paid money to assassinate him. Any agent with a resume like his would have been a target. His survival gave testament to his skill.

Eyes the color of sheet metal stared at the window, unseeing. Small imperfections marred a handsome face: a slight curve of his nose where it had broken, a small scar on his chin. A line of white scar tissue split a brown eyebrow. He'd done more than evade these criminals; he'd fought them.

"You should've taken him up on his offer," he said quietly.

Brody, he meant. Had he heard the low conversation we'd exchanged? Or did he just deduce what was being said? It didn't matter.

"I'm not interested in his offer. I want this case."

"You have no idea what this case is even about, rookie."

Questions sat on the tip of my tongue. *So what's the case about, then? When can we get started?* But only one came out.

"What happened to the last guy?"

That finally got his full attention. He looked at me, and I felt the gaze of his gunmetal eyes like a blow. It stole my breath and rendered me speechless. He looked me up and down. His mouth set in a flat line, unimpressed by my gender, my youth, or maybe the pink blouse I wore. Whatever he saw, it made him answer.

"He died. The last time I went after Carlos Laguardia, my partner died. A punk kid who thought he could bring down a monster."

His words and his tone challenged me. *Run away,* they said. But I heard the desolation beneath the warning. Whatever family or friends the *punk kid* might have had, this man had mourned him. Hennessy might be a ruthless agent, but he cared about his partners.

I extended my hand. "Then let's get the bastard

responsible."

His eyes widened minutely, the faintest indication I'd surprised him before the cynical mask snapped back into place. He studied me, gauging my sincerity, my intelligence, or whatever resemblance I might have borne to the punk kid. I could see him judging my pearl earrings and the unfortunately youthful button nose on my face and finding me lacking. Most guys assumed I couldn't fight. I had my second Dan in Tae Kwon Do, and I was a better shot than the rest of my graduating class. I was freaking competent, and if this guy was going to question it, if he was going to be prejudiced and—

He nodded. Curtly. Decisively. His approval washed over me, warming me in a way that even Brody's hadn't. This guy was the real deal, the Lone Ranger of the country's gangland, and I'd gladly be his trusty sidekick.

He accepted my hand and awareness rose from where his skin heated mine. Awareness that he was a man, that he was a handsome one. I sensed an answering ripple go through him, as if he'd just registered me as a woman. Attraction, plain and simple. A chemical reaction, really.

I pushed it aside.

Besides that, a different kind of alertness had begun to move through me, one that had nothing to do with the lean muscled body in front of me. This assignment was real. The biggest case to come through our branch in the time I'd been here, and I'd just been assigned as a principal agent. Holy shit. I carefully schooled my expression, forcing back the giddiness. I didn't even care about whatever ulterior motives they might have had.

For surely there had been ulterior motives. A hundred other agents were more qualified for the role on this floor alone. It didn't matter. If I contributed one tiny thing that led to us bringing down Laguardia, I'd make a name for myself. No more schlepping coffee or making copies. But my desire ran even deeper than that. Even darker. The sinister excitement I'd felt when I'd held my father's life in my hands, when I'd turned him in—I felt it now too. It hummed through me, sleek and dark in my veins.

"What are we going to do first?" I asked Hennessey, my voice coming out breathless. I hoped he didn't notice the flush on my cheeks or my rapid pulse of excitement. The way his gaze flicked to the base of my neck and then away said my hope was in vain.

"First, you're going to study the case files. I'm already familiar, so I'll go ahead and do the questioning."

"Questioning?"

"An inmate. They're holding him down at the courthouse for his arraignment, and I need to speak with him."

A shiny laminate "Visitor" badge was clipped to his lapel. Despite his impressive credentials and senior rank, he was an outsider in this office. As a rookie, so was I.

"We," I corrected.

"Pardon?"

"*We* need to speak with him. I've already read the case files. I *do* know what this case is about. And I'm coming with you."

He radiated suspicion, as if he'd never heard of initiative and had never seen anyone be assertive. "Why would you read case files if you didn't know you'd get assigned here?"

"Because I ran out of money to buy more detective novels. Why do you think?" I blew out a breath, shocked at myself. What the hell? Being sarcastic wasn't the way to make friends. Then again, there was little chance of Hennessey being my friend. He didn't want me as a partner. He barely registered my existence.

Though, he registered me now. His eyes narrowed, his lips firmed. He wasn't happy, but I couldn't be sorry. His gray eyes took my measure, as more than an annoying new girl, as more than a woman—as an equal. "So you feel confident with the case? With Laguardia?"

"Yes, sir."

"State his full name."

"Carlos Frederico Laguardia." I continued to recite the next ten most commonly used aliases. We had no idea what his real birth name had been. Even his identity was a fabrication, a fraud like the disguises and the pretend trips.

If I'd expected Hennessey to be impressed with my recitation, I'd have been disappointed. He frowned. "Where was he last seen?"

"Switzerland." I paused, wondering how much I should say. How much to reveal to a partner who didn't yet trust me. "At least, that's what the official reports say.

But it wasn't him."

One brow rose. "Explain."

His stern command sent a shiver down my spine. That autocratic tone annoyed me, but I couldn't deny he'd earned the right to use it. He had so much more experience, more skills than I. Where did I get off telling him he was wrong? Still, I'd pulled the lever to my own trap door by opening my mouth. The only thing left to do was fall through it.

I thought back to the world map pinned on the wall, the pins in all the reliable sightings, the yarn connecting them loose and drooping to the floor like streamers in a party long over.

"He doesn't like the cold," I finally said.

The silence grew thick and potent. "He doesn't like the cold?"

I shifted uncomfortably. "He avoids it. His head-quarters have always been in warm locations. Mexico. South America. The one in North Africa."

"The Algerian compound was never confirmed. And Mexico… South America… It didn't occur to you that those are the major centers of drug and weapons trafficking?" He looked incredulous.

"And Russia," I said quietly. My chest felt tight. I wished I'd never started this. "Russia is another major center of drug and weapon trafficking, but he never goes there." *Because it's cold.*

He stared at me as if I'd lost my mind. And maybe I had. Maybe that had happened years ago and neither the court-appointed psychiatrist nor the FBI staff who'd cleared me for duty had ever noticed.

Hennessey barked a laugh. "Jesus. You know, the Russians prefer human trafficking these days, having more people than drugs or weapons. And maybe Laguardia just doesn't like the Gulag. But I take your point." He laughed again, as if in disbelief. "It's a fair theory, and a new one, I'll give you that much."

The knot loosened inside me, letting me breathe again. He might suspect I was crazy, but at least he knew I paid attention. I could be an asset to him.

A new, grudging respect lightened his eyes, turning them silver. "Okay, rookie, you can come. But I'm driving."

I didn't bother hiding my smile. I didn't care who drove, and besides, that was to be expected. I doubted this man ever gave up much control. I bet his commands extended into the bedroom. The thought filled me with unexpected, unwelcome heat.

CHAPTER TWO

WHAT DO YOU remember? Such an open-ended question.

I remembered going to prison exactly three times.

A few months back, when I had just started, Brody had brought me along to take notes on an interview in a half-hearted attempt at mentorship. The subject had been a long-term inmate in a low security prison who received cigarettes in exchange for intel—or more accurately, prison gossip. The exchange had been concise and boring. My notes, when I had submitted them for the case file, had been the same.

That was the third time I'd been to prison.

Before that, I'd gone on something like a field trip at Quantico. Each of us had been assigned a convict. We studied their crimes beforehand, the evidence and the trials. Then we visited them and added in-person assessments to our reports. My inmate had been a bank fraud expert, a real nice guy with age spots and two grandkids in Detroit. He showed me pictures and asked me to pass along a letter. I reported his illegal request to the board. If assholes like that wanted to fuck around with the law, then they didn't deserve the children or grandchildren they'd been given. I was doing those kids a favor.

That was two.

But the first time I'd ever been to prison, I was ten years old. By then, my father had been inside for two months with good behavior, no violent incidents. He'd placed a request for visitation of his only child, and the court had somehow agreed. My foster mother at the time had put me in a dress with pink and orange flowers and white patent leather shoes. I remembered how shiny they looked compared to the dark concrete floor. I remembered how they looked covered in blood.

My father tried to kill me that day. Prison security was different back then, less high-tech and more dependent on a guard with a baton. My father had come at me with his fists like a bludgeon, wrists and ankles still handcuffed together. The guard stepped in quickly, beating my father half to death. I'd huddled in the corner, staring at the red ink splatter on my shoes and feeling an odd sense of triumph. He'd broken my arm and given me a black eye, but I got to walk out of there. He didn't.

He had already been serving twenty years, a plea bargain combining all his crimes, but the assault on me had tipped him over into a lifer. He'd never draw a free breath again, and most days, I didn't care at all.

These three visits played over in my head, like forlorn notes to an old remembered song. Just as well, because Hennessey didn't turn on the radio. The jail in question was ten miles from FBI headquarters, but in downtown Houston near lunch hour, the drive would take twenty minutes, easy.

Hennessey's fingers drummed on the steering wheel as the car rolled forward at ten miles per hour in heavy traffic.

"So," I began quietly, "why the big push for Laguardia in Houston?" At his questioning look, I continued, "I know you've been stationed in New York. The Di Mariano family. The Mencia heist. They're both up there. And the New York office is pretty big. I figure you would have worked the case from there, unless you think he's in the area."

I couldn't see his eyes beneath the aviator sunglasses he wore, but the side of his lip quirked up. "Well, yeah, you know how he feels about the cold. He's probably sunbathing in Galveston right now."

Even though he was mocking me, a small laugh bubbled up. I tamped it down, ruthless, shrugging instead. "Fine, don't tell me."

There was a pause, as if he were debating how much to say. I suspected he usually operated this way, portioning out his words, measuring how much information to give and how much to keep hidden. What would it be like to be in this man's confidence? It seemed like an impossible dream. This man gathered information; he didn't give it away.

A brief nod said he'd found his answer. "He's planning a big shipment. Drugs. Probably in through the

Gulf."

"How do you know?"

"There's been chatter," he said vaguely.

I didn't push. Partly because I suspected he wouldn't tell me. And partly because I'd learned that the FBI's methods of intel weren't always that impressive. An image of the reedy informant Brody had interviewed flashed through my mind. I hadn't gotten the impression he was lying, but how much were a few packs of cigarettes worth anyway? We relied on the integrity of men who had none, but it was the only way. Without their false promises, we had nothing at all.

"This guy we're going to see. He knows about the shipment?"

"He knows that it's happening. It remains to be seen how many details he has."

"What makes you think he's going to share? That's got to be worth more than cigarettes or booze. Laguardia may kill him if he finds out this guy talked."

"Sure, I may not get much, but I have to follow the leads. Shake the trees and see what falls out."

Ah, the scientific method of law enforcement. I narrowed my eyes in suspicion. "And I'm going to participate in this tree-shaking, right?"

"You'll watch," he corrected, and for unknown reasons, I blushed. Thankfully, he was staring at the road from behind tinted glasses, so my inappropriate reaction went unnoticed.

"Inside the room." I had no plans to sit behind a

one-way mirror.

"Fine. But you stay quiet. No matter what happens. Got it, rookie?"

"Got it." I wasn't scared. The security nowadays was ten thousand times better than ten years ago. I was an adult now, a trained agent. *Dark red liquid splattered on shiny white leather.* "You don't expect anything to happen, though. He's not violent, right?"

Hennessey turned and stared, his gaze intense even blocked by his glasses. I could sense him peeling back the layers that I'd thought were impenetrable. He was a damn good investigator, obviously, and his ability to discern the truth wasn't restricted to the criminals we interrogated.

Without speaking, he turned into a parking garage and flashed his badge to the guard. We circled the levels, climbing higher to find a free space. By the time he parked and shut off the ignition, I'd resigned myself to not getting an answer. Maybe we'd let the question, and my moment of cowardice, pass like a rhetorical question—a random discordant note in the flow of conversation.

He didn't step out of the car, and when I reached for the door, he put his hand on my arm to stop me. I faced him, shocked anew by the silver eyes he revealed as he took off his sunglasses. They were striated with darker lines that varied with his thoughts, mercurial and completely opaque, like studying the sky for clues only to be caught in the storm.

"Every criminal, every man, every woman can be dangerous," he said, "if their back's against the wall. If you're standing between them and something they want, you're the enemy. Pretending otherwise, pretending you can be *safe*, is just a way to get yourself killed."

"Okay," I breathed, wondering how much he was revealing about himself, about how *he'd* been hurt with this advice meant for me.

"But nothing's going to happen inside, because we're not going to let it. We have the power. We have control of the situation. You're going to sit quietly and not draw his attention. I'm going to ask questions. We'll be back in this car in twenty minutes. Got it?"

Relief swept through my veins. "Got it."

I exited the car and followed him with a lightness in my step...and a new curiosity about the man in front of me. He both alarmed and comforted me. I didn't understand it, but I felt safe when he was near.

Some of my confidence began to slip as we went through three separate bar enclosures to get to the interview room. Double guards were stationed at each level. We had to surrender all of our belongings, even the pen and pad I'd brought for taking notes. I'd never been this deep before, but this seemed extreme. Like beyond high security, designed to keep people out as much as in. After all, Laguardia would want to get inside if he could. To kill this guy before he could tell us what he knew. The bars and protocols protected the people inside as much as the ones out.

The final door was an extra-wide metal door with a small square window too high for me to see through in my low heels. The guard stationed beside it moved to open the handle, but Hennessey held up his hand.

He spoke low, for my ears only. "When we're in there, no talking. No smiling. Don't react to what he says in any way."

"Ah," I said with exaggerated understanding. "You want to play good cop/bad cop."

He frowned. "No, absolutely not. I said—"

"Kidding, Hennessey. Still and silent, got it."

One eyebrow rose. "This isn't a game."

"Then stop treating me like I'm on my first police ride along. I was top of my class at Quantico. I may not be The Great Ian Hennessey, but I'm not going to fuck this up."

He stared at me, his expression inscrutable. Then his face eased just a fraction. Something shifted in the air between us, trust falling into its groove the way it should between partners. Real partners.

"It was funny, the good cop/bad cop thing," he conceded. Then he nodded to the guard and stepped into the room.

I snorted to myself. *It was funny,* he'd said with a totally straight face. What would it take to make him crack a smile? Or make him laugh? It shouldn't have mattered, but I resolved to find out. Like picking up clues and uncovering a person's secrets, I would solve the puzzle of Ian Hennessy.

The door closed behind me with an ominous clang. Locked in. We didn't just visit the prisoners; we became them for these few minutes, closed in, guarded against escape. It was a mindset encouraged by the bare walls and metal table. By the temperature dropping ten degrees, passing comfortably cool and going straight to chilled. The fluorescent lights flickered almost imperceptibly, making it seem as if we were underwater, a cave with strangely-shaped fish that carried little lanterns in front of their faces, the better to eat you with.

A windblown Santa Claus sat on a metal chair, his snow-colored beard long and crinkly. That was my first impression, and the orange jumpsuit did little to dispel his genial appearance. It was only when he turned to me that I saw his face, the way the scar tissue furled in on his eyes, threatening to close them. It wouldn't have made any difference if it had; his eyes were a glassy blue, unseeing.

Daniel Fuentes was blind.

One of the only men in custody who'd ever seen Laguardia, and he wouldn't be able to describe him. A coincidence? I couldn't believe that. I suspected he was still alive, not because of the twenty guards we'd passed between the entrance and here, but because he couldn't identify Laguardia.

Fuck.

Hennessey didn't seem fazed by this new development. He'd probably already known about the man's blindness when he set up the interview.

"Who's the bitch?" Fuentes grunted.

Charming. And creepy, considering he couldn't see me. Sharpened sense of hearing, I guessed. Hennessy smoothly pulled out a chair and nodded, directing me to sit. I sat.

"Agent Holmes will be attending this interview. I'm Agent Ian Hennessey."

"And I'm Mother Fucking Theresa. What do you want from me?"

Hennessy didn't even blink. The other man couldn't see him, but his expression was smooth as silk, as if he sat in front of a busy courtroom, a poker face. Now I understood why he'd told me not to smile. The urge to laugh bubbled up in me from some previously untapped spring, a combination of nerves and latent appreciation of the absurdity of the situation.

A blind coke-head Santa Clause in an orange suit sitting across from the crisply-starched renowned Ian Hennessey. My life was surreal, but then what else was new? When I was seven years old, I'd woken up from a bad dream and gone looking for my father. He'd been washing blood off his hands in the sink, and he'd steered me back to bed.

He'd *touched* my shoulder with the blood of another child, and I'd fallen into a kind of terrified trance. I'd never woken up, not even when he'd been put in jail, not even when he attacked me there. Everything had always felt wavering and unreal, and the shuddering lights in this room only emphasized it. *This is my life. I'll never wake up.*

Hennessey asked him the standard questions. Where were you on this date or that? Do you have any knowledge of drug activity, of shipments? Bullshit answers. Curse words. Fuentes called Hennessey's mom a fat slut pig who he fucked in the skull, and Hennessey asked, in a voice so casual and smooth, if he'd ever met a man known as Carlos Laguardia.

Fuentes stiffened. He tried to hide his reaction, but I saw it.

Hennessey did too. He leaned forward. "When?"

Fuentes kicked back suddenly, almost toppling backward, letting loose a stream of rapid-fire Spanish swear words. I jumped at the sudden movement, ruining my statue imitation. Hennessey just looked at him, as if faintly curious, like watching the movements of ants on a park bench.

The man didn't look like Santa anymore. His eyes rolled around, landing on nothing. He panted, the wild hair like foam at the mouth. "You can't make me say nothing. You can't fucking make me. I'm not going to die."

His fear was infectious; it filled the room, an airborne pathogen. I caught it, breathed it in. My pulse raced, my palms sweated. Even the unmovable Hennessey shifted in his seat, as if he felt a fourth presence in the room, a ghost standing beside the table. *Carlos Laguardia.*

"You're safe here," Hennessey said. "I can protect you."

"Fuck you," Fuentes spat. "You fucking *hijo de puta* motherfucker with your fucking badge, thinking you own everyone. Thinking you control everyone. Well, you don't control me, and you can't make me talk."

"I can protect you," Hennessey repeated. "But only if you help me. Otherwise you're just another inmate. What can I do about that?" He turned to me, then, as if he expected me to answer. I stared back, wide-eyed. He continued, "I can't do anything to help a man charged with your crimes, a guilty man. But if you helped me, right now, I would make a call—"

"No." Anxiety thickened Fuentes's voice. "No calls. No calls."

I couldn't even blame him. Carlos had friends in supposedly safe places. Cops. Security guards. Who's to say he didn't have a friend in the Witness Protection Program?

But his fear proved one thing: he knew something. Something useful, something he wasn't telling us. Hennessey knew it too. His gray eyes glinted with renewed purpose.

Hennessey's voice lowered, soothing and almost seductive. "Fuentes, I want to help you. But I need to know you're on my side. I have to know that I can trust you."

Fuentes moaned, rocking slightly in his chair. Animal sounds filled the room. His chair clattered against the concrete floor. My heart crawled up into my throat. This was real fear, like the shadow of a memory, something

I'd been running from for a long time.

I'd been frozen the first time I'd seen blood on my father's hands, the first time he'd touched it to my cheek and wished me goodnight. *What do you remember?* I was broken inside, a psychotic break at age six that I'd been so careful to hide from the world. I never knew emotions the way other people did. I didn't have morals, and I found his fear so cold, so alluring. I wanted to touch it, to place my palm against the frosted glass and leave a handprint behind.

I'd only ever wanted to be normal, prayed for it, but it had always been too late for me. While other children had backed away from white vans, I'd looked at them with longing. I wanted to be special enough to be taken. I wanted to matter that much.

"Just give us something, a show of faith," Hennessey continued, relentless.

"Why don't you ask Carlos's *puta*, huh? The bitch lives here, right? Married one of your fucking badges, didn't she?"

I remembered reading about the woman Carlos had kept around for obvious reasons. She'd turned on him and managed to escape alive.

So it was possible.

Hennessey was inexorable. "I'm asking *you*. Or I might let it slip that you *did* tell us something. I bet some people wouldn't be happy about that."

His threat rang in the air, shocking me. Did we do that? Did we threaten to do something that would have an inmate killed? Would he follow through with it?

Fuentes shook his head, muttering nonsense words, a tie-dye language of English and Spanish and stilted ghetto slang I knew from my childhood.

It was too late for him. He was blind and broken and locked in one of the tightest security holds that existed. He had a hundred charges against him. If he got out, he would have to face Laguardia. He had no hope, but if there was one thing he could do, if there was one man who had the power to change this man's fate...

"Tell him," I said. My voice came out rusty, as if it had been hours since I'd last spoken instead of minutes. "Please, give him some information. About the shipment, anything. Maybe it won't even matter. They'll change it anyway, now that they know you're caught. It doesn't have to be useful to get you into the program. It just has to be the truth. Something you heard."

Hennessey looked fit to kill. Me, to be exact. His glare accused me. *I told you to stay quiet. You said you would.* I shrugged slightly, not sorry. Even if it didn't help, it couldn't hurt.

Except Fuentes's gaze narrowed on me as if he could see my face. In his pale flat eyes I saw a flicker of recognition. A chill went down my spine, and I wondered for a terrifying moment if his blindness was faked. The doctors in prison had ways of checking that, didn't they? I had no idea, but God, that would be a pretty slick way to get information when people didn't think you could.

When I spoke again, it was quieter. "Tell us something you heard. Something you saw."

He blinked, a hint of confusion on his face. It was believable, that was for sure. But then, he was a liar and a murderer. I'd learned long ago not to trust men like him.

I'd learned not to trust anyone. I still didn't want him to die.

"Please," I murmured.

He continued to stare at me, but I felt his voice directed at Hennessey. "Fifteen minutes with her. You step outside."

The chill in my body turned into a deep freeze. He was asking for fifteen minutes alone…with me. I stared at Fuentes, unable to comprehend what he'd asked. So seriously, too, as if he really thought it might happen. Even though it wouldn't. I glanced at Hennessey to be sure.

My new partner met my gaze, and I felt a cold stab of fear. Real fear, the kind I had always been reaching for. His eyes held scales, weighing the information we could get against leaving me with Fuentes for fifteen minutes. Weighing precious information against a rookie agent. The perverted scales of justice, and they tilted against me.

"Five," Hennessey said.

My heart turned into a thunderstorm, heavy and untamed. Oh God. This couldn't be happening. It was a dream, the horrible trance. *Wake up, wake up.*

Fuentes snorted. "What could I do in five minutes?

Barely stand up. Nothing. *Nada*."

Feeling off balance, I stood up. My chair scraped against the floor, filling the room with an awful screech, like the scream I was incapable of making.

"Ten minutes," Fuentes countered.

Hennessey stood up too, and I walked backward until the cold wall stopped me, imprinting its cracks on my body. How far would he go to get the information he needed? How far would he go to bring down a criminal? Was *this* how he'd managed to catch so many of them? But Hennessey wasn't walking toward me. He circled the table, going for Fuentes.

Fuentes backed up too, knocking over his chair. We shared a kinship in that moment, both of us terrified of Hennessey but tied to him. Like planets orbiting the sun, we needed him for survival, but we would keep our distance as long as we could. Fuentes huddled against the wall, looking pathetic even though he was larger, slightly taller and definitely wider, than Hennessey. Still, Hennessey managed to put his palms on either side of the other man's head. He leaned over him, threatening him without a single touch.

"I'll leave you alone with her, but it will take less than five minutes. You're old and handcuffed, and I'm not talking about a quick fuck anyway. I'm talking about how long it'll take for her to kill you once I give her a knife and tell her what you did to those three little girls in Tijuana. Or was it four? You'd know better than me."

Fuentes was shaking. I was shaking. The world felt

unsteady, an earthquake in our heads. Three little girls in Tijuana.

What do you remember?

I remembered rage. The impotent rage of a child. Fuentes disgusted me, but the worst part of all was that I connected with him. He looked past Hennessey's shoulder and stared into my eyes because he felt it too. I believed he was blind in that moment, because this wasn't a man who would want to be weaker than he already was. He heard my breathing, he felt my pain, and he homed in on it. I wanted that knife. I wanted to use it. Did Hennessey know that about me? Could he tell?

Five minutes. Ten. What could happen in fifteen minutes?

"Two weeks from now," Fuentes said, wheezing. "In two weeks. There's a building shaped like an M. An old warehouse nobody uses owned by Laguardia under a shell corporation. That's where the drugs are going. A lot of them." Fuentes slumped against the wall, defeated. "That's all I can tell you."

Hennessey stepped back and straightened his suit. "Thank you."

Fuentes slid down to the floor, the orange fabric stretching grotesquely across his legs and belly. "The call?" he asked, sounding like a lost child. "You'll make the call."

Hennessey nodded shortly. "I will."

Fuentes nodded, looking miserable. Guilt over ratting out Laguardia? Or fear for himself?

When my legs would support me again, I pushed off the wall and followed Hennessey out of the room. We walked in silence, with only the accompaniment of metal bars clanging to mark the steps. Even when the sunlight blinded my eyes and the exhaust of the city burned my lungs, I stayed silent. Mute. Like he'd told me to be inside. Why hadn't I listened?

This will be our little secret, okay?

That was what my father had told me, but I hadn't listened to him either. I just couldn't keep quiet, even when it was important. I was constantly searching, always reaching out, desperate for a connection that I had yet to find.

My poise lasted until we reached his car in the parking garage. He went to the driver's side door, but instead of getting inside, I went to stand by the wall, resting my forehead against the cool cement. Like the walls of the interview room and yet so different. Here we were free, with the sunlight streaming in through open-air spaces on the sides. Here we were safe. Tears streamed down my cheeks, as unstoppable as rain.

I felt Hennessey behind me, and then he was turning me, pulling me close. I breathed in his scent and sank into the hardness of his embrace. I climbed inside him, standing still, while he held me, murmuring words I couldn't understand. The cloth of his dress shirt became wet beneath my cheek, damp with tears, the transference of fear from me to him, because he was strong enough to carry the burden for both of us. *Are you afraid?* No. Not with him.

"Sorry," I mumbled. Sorry for crying on you. Sorry I spoke in the room when I wasn't supposed to. Sorry I'm a weak, inexperienced rookie you're stuck with.

"I wanted to spare you that," Hennessey said gruffly. Meaning a direct confrontation with the man. I'd brought it on myself, he meant.

"It's okay. I knew you wouldn't really do it, what he asked for."

The statement hung in the air like a question. I wanted reassurance, after that one breathless moment when I'd thought he was seriously negotiating my rape.

Hennessey didn't have any reassurance for me. "Fuentes gave us what we needed."

"And you're going to…to make the call, right? For witness protection?" I didn't know why I cared about a criminal. He'd probably done lots of horrible things, and I had no desire to learn the details of the girls in Tijuana. Yet it felt important that we follow through on the promise we'd made. Because for a moment, it had seemed as though the threat Hennessey had made to Fuentes was real too, spreading the word that he had talked and thus ensuring his death. Hennessey had sounded so horribly sincere, and I wanted to believe it was the mark of a great interrogator.

Hennessey stepped back, his hands lingering on my arms a second too long. He spoke softly, with something like regret in his eyes. "You have to understand. He's already dead. From the moment we stepped into the room. Laguardia won't care if he talked or not. He's a liability. From the moment he did business with a man like that, this is how it had to be."

It was my first glimpse of how this game really worked, outside of the weird bubble my father had created, outside of the carefully manicured lectures in the academy. In the real crime world, everyone was a target. We were all going to die here; it was just a question of when and how gruesome it would be.

Only as we pulled away did I realize what was strange about that room. I pictured it again in my mind. Drab walls butted up against each other, with a flat ceiling stacked on top. There was no camera in that room. No mirrored window with an observation room on the other side. No evidence that Hennessey had ever threatened Fuentes, except for my word. And if Hennessey had left me in that room for five, ten, fifteen minutes, if he'd gotten the guard outside to agree, there would've been no evidence of that either.

CHAPTER THREE

THE NEXT MORNING, I woke up before my alarm went off. The sky outside was stained pink, like someone had washed something red with the pale sheet of sky.

I wore my silk blouse with the pale yellow chevron patterns that I'd found at a vintage shop on a rare trip to Austin. Over that I wore a black jacket far too rigid to really be comfortable. I didn't like it, but it was basically a requirement to be taken seriously. I was already a rookie, and my short height and china doll features didn't do me any favors.

So I put on the sleek Italian wool, but underneath it all, I wore satin and lace and remembered the feel of a warm, solid chest beneath my cheek. I wished I could take back that moment, so he would see me as an equal instead of a scared little girl.

No, scratch that. I wanted him to remember that moment like I would, one second of the connection I'd always been searching for. I hoped my tears had stained his shirt, turning it a grim impossible pink so he would remember I was a woman too. I'd always been ancient, really—even when I was a kid.

I drove to work wondering how just one day could make things seem a little sharper, a little weightier. Was it Hennessey who made it different? Or was it the act of facing evil for the first time in over a decade?

Both, maybe.

Life or death situations could bind you to a stranger, the way I mourned every day for the children my father killed. For the children I'd *let* him kill before I turned him in. We were in the same position, those kids and me. At the mercy of a psychopath. But they had died, and I had lived.

Survivor's guilt, the textbook would say. It wasn't me who had caused that pain; it was misfortune, coincidence, the melody of a madman. I was a victim too, they said. I was the one who had suffered, not the one who caused suffering. Except I hadn't ever suffered, not really. No one had ever hit me or continued to touch me when I said no.

Creepy men in white vans took one look at the jaded knowledge in my eyes and kept on driving. They knew there was no innocence left to corrupt—just a hollowed out space where my soul should have been.

I didn't want those men to hurt me because I liked pain. I wanted them to hurt me because I knew I deserved it all along. I'd escaped it through a twist of fate. I'd let the hurt fall to other more hopeful children. And for that, I would always deserve to be punished.

Hennessey was leaning against his car when I pulled up. Morning light glinted off his smooth jaw. He seemed somehow younger than before. He looked bright and put together, as if yesterday's stress and upheaval had meant nothing to him. Threatening a child molester with death was like fetching coffee for him. Implying he might let his rookie partner get raped was like filing a paper. Part of the job, easy peasy.

He nodded toward the passenger side. "Get in, rookie."

"Where are we going?"

"To catch a bad guy. Where else?"

His voice was light, and I took that airiness into myself. I made it mine. Let this be a joke. At least then I could be in on it. *A coping mechanism,* the textbook would say. Life was one big coping mechanism, one more beat passing without desperation, another moment without fear. I wasn't afraid of a joke.

We didn't go back to the prison. Instead, we went to the permitting center and rode a creaky elevator to the fifth floor. A large dusty room contained architectural plans and permits for the entire city, in no sort of order that made sense to me. There were gaps, too, I learned. With a building changing from one survey to the next without any official construction permit being filed. The thin fading carbon copies chronicled the growth of a metropolis, only hinting at the people who lived within it.

And I found that looking for a building near the docks shaped like an M was fucking hard. We found a seemingly endless amount of possibilities, and we set each one aside so we could check into its current usage and ownership. And the worst part was knowing we could miss it in this haphazard pile. The proverbial M-shaped needle in the biggest haystack in Texas. For all the fancy gadgetry we oohed and ahhed over in the academy, actual detective work was a backward business. We peered into the past, hoping it would help. But history held on to its secrets like a forest at night, shrouded in moonlight and steeped in folklore. There was magic in these dusty volumes, but all we could see were shadows.

We walked over to a diner for lunch, where I ordered a salad and two eggs sunny side up. Hennessey ordered a burger loaded with cheese and bacon, fries, and a milkshake. I raised my eyebrows as the waitress left us.

Hennessey grinned, almost boyish. "Sorry, I don't share. You'll have to get your own if you get tired of rabbit food."

I snorted. "My arteries will thank me later."

"You're not into living dangerously?"

"I'm an FBI agent working one of the highest profile cases south of the Mason Dixon. My danger quota is full."

He nodded, turning pensive. "You're probably right. Though sometimes…it gets to be too much, to live a normal life with a dangerous job. We build up all this steam, and we don't have the release of money and drugs the way the criminals do."

"Maybe you don't," I deadpanned, and he laughed.

His smile changed his whole face, made him younger and so handsome that my heart squeezed. Synapses lit up in my brain, firing into places long asleep. Like waking up and finding the world more vivid than your dreams.

His smile faded. He looked me in the eye. "Truth is, I never planned to live very long. In this job, there's always a bullet out there with my name on it."

I looked down, tracing a groove in the laminate with my fingernail. Not a grown up response, but it was all I could manage in that moment. I had the sense of a ghost again, of Carlos Laguardia and a hundred other criminals, all gathered around us with sinister incorporeal faces.

Since I was in this job too, there was a bullet with *my* name on it. But that didn't bother me. That was why I was here, if I were being honest. Some criminals sought their deaths using *suicide by cop*. Me? I'd been working at *suicide by criminal* my whole broken life.

But if Hennessey were killed…that would hurt. He was a larger-than-life hero in my mind, his death unthinkable to me.

I never planned to live very long. His words chilled me.

Trying to break the somber mood, I quipped, "I hate to break it to you, but you're no spring chicken. You've already lived a long time."

It worked. He quirked a grin, and my insides lurched forward, speeding up again. It was like riding a high, teasing out those smiles of his, and if I wasn't careful, I could become addicted.

His eyes twinkled. "So maybe you can start looking out for me, partner. Watch what I eat."

"Maybe," I said, missing the word *rookie* coming out of his mouth, realizing his voice had been laced with strange affection each time. *Partner* sounded respectful and cold falling from his lips.

"We'll spend the rest of the day in the record room," he said, switching subjects. "That should be enough to get us started. We can dig into the backgrounds tomorrow."

"Okay." A question hovered on my tongue. "Doesn't it seem kind of...random? Hoping he's telling us the truth and assuming we'll find the right building and be able to tell that it is. There's so many ways for it to go wrong."

His eyes were grave as he nodded, and I appreciated that he took my question seriously. "It's true, but crime is random. The nature of detective work is to always be one step behind. We have to wait until they commit a crime or make a mistake, and then we can follow them."

One step behind. How accurate. How depressing. I stared at him, realizing how difficult that might be for a man with pride. With initiative. How much easier it'd be as a criminal, how freeing.

He continued, "And then one day, we catch up. We get some commendations, and we move on to the next case."

"If crime is random, I take it you don't believe in

trying to understand the criminals, the way their mind works, why they do what they do."

"Nah, I leave that to the doctors. And the lawyers. My job is to put them in handcuffs. That's all I allow myself to care about, because as often as not, they end up back on the streets with a plea bargain or whatever the fuck."

"You paint a bleak picture, Hennessey."

"Just being honest, rookie."

I warmed at the return of his endearment. That was what it had become now, an expression of kindness. He had grieved for the other rookie who had died. It meant something to him, to be young and new here. He wanted me to live, to succeed, and that elevated my junior status to a place of honor.

"Are we going to do what Fuentes said and interview Laguardia's woman?" The word fell awkwardly from my lips, but I didn't want to call her a *puta* or a whore. I wasn't really sure who she'd been to Laguardia except that she'd fucked him. There'd been a few pages about her in the files, but they'd been mostly blacked out, unreadable. Classified. Since she'd gotten away, I assumed she'd flipped on Laguardia. Except that didn't explain why she was still alive. Carlos wouldn't let a betrayal go unpunished...but he had, with her.

Hennessy shook his head. "That was years ago. She won't have any information on this deal going down or his current whereabouts."

She knew *something*. The blacked-out pages proved

that.

"We can ask her general questions. Like what Laguardia looks like. She slept with him. She should at least know that much."

A grainy black-and-white image flashed through my mind, of a man standing still in a crowd, looking up. He wore a large jacket—was it required to cover him or was it part of the disguise?

Hennessey looked bored. "Five-foot-ten. A hundred and eighty pounds. Black hair, strong build. Like a million other criminals."

"She might know the way he works. His quirks. Whether he usually attends important shipments like this one and what role he might play."

Hennessey gave me a faintly pitying look, and his voice, when he spoke, was gentler. "These kinds of guys don't let their women participate in business. They don't treat them as equals."

Like we do, was the subtext. But even there, it wasn't true. Women didn't advance at the same rate as men in the FBI. They weren't, on average, paid as much. Even my position on this case was an unexplained thing with an ulterior motive lurking somewhere out of reach. Equality was a pipe dream on either side of the law, and it made me defensive.

"That's exactly my point. They wouldn't have believed her capable of anything, so they wouldn't have guarded themselves around her. She could have overheard things. She could be a gold mine of information."

I was breathing hard, somehow. Sweating, as if this had become a fight. Hennessey stared at me in the same way he had at Fuentes, like looking down at ants, like wondering at the strange behavior of lesser mortals. Suddenly this diner table was metal to match his eyes, the retro décor around us turned to concrete walls. The dim sound of voices evened out into the buzz of fluorescent lights, no other people here, no cameras, no witnesses.

He spoke in the same even voice he'd used in that room, low and seductive. "You want to know what information she has for us? Whether he liked to give it to her in the pussy or in the ass. How rough did his blowjobs get and does he pay extra if she bleeds."

I stared at him, unblinking. I couldn't believe he was talking to me like this, except I'd asked for it, hadn't I? I'd pushed him, and now he was pushing back. His words felt like a threat, and I wore an orange jumpsuit and handcuffs, headed for certain death. Trapped.

"That's how women get treated by men like Laguardia. That's the part they gloss over in the academy textbooks."

That's why we're going to stop them, I willed him to say, desperate to redeem the man in front of me. We were on the same side, but in that moment, he felt like my enemy. In that moment, I saw my future. Even worse, I saw a glimmer of amusement in his eyes. The smug expression of an animal who'd spotted his prey—and knew he would catch her.

Then he sat back. The illusion lifted.

I heard the clatter of silverware clang in my ears, felt the lamp swing above our table, too bright. I took a breath and felt it spread through my lungs like acid. His expression had returned to its usual, half-sardonic, half-distracted. He looked endearingly rumpled and slightly apologetic.

God, I was crazy, imagining bad guys everywhere, all around.

"Sorry," Hennessey said. "I'm going to have to pull rank on this one. If we were desperate for leads, maybe. What we really need is more time to go through all these records, to find where the deal is going down and start laying down surveillance."

At least he seemed genuinely regretful, and it *was* a valid reason. The woman could be a wild goose chase, a waste of time like he thought. Then again, she might know the most important things of all. One thing Hennessey didn't seem to realize was that it said a lot about a man whether he preferred to give it in the pussy or in the ass and how he liked his blowjobs. It exposed a man too, when he made a woman bleed.

CHAPTER FOUR

ENNESSEY HADN'T BEEN kidding about the amount of work required to find the building. Even Lance got roped into the research.

"What's field work like?" he asked me back in the office.

If I remembered the few moments in the interview room, field work was terrifying. It sat in a gray area, where right and wrong blended into one directive: results. But I tried not to remember the time in the interview room. Something about it twisted me inside, tied me in knots I could never untangle with Bureau rules and regulations.

"It's a lot like this," I answered him, referring to the stacks of architectural plans and permits covering every inch of the cherrywood conference table. "Not very glamorous."

Which was the truth, at least. Making a blind man piss himself didn't factor into any glossy movie screen version of detective work.

I expected Hennessey to leave the grunt work to us rookies, but he stayed with us, sleeves rolled up. He sat beside us from 6:00 a.m., when we stumbled in, groping for a mug of coffee, until 8:00 p.m., when we drained the last cold dregs of brownish liquid from the machine and dragged ourselves home. It may not have been glamorous work, sorting through paperwork, but it was a very real part of the job that would save lives. If we found the place in time. Our administrative treasure hunt had a ticking clock.

"You can go," I offered him, when Lance had left the room to get us all coffee. "If you have something more important to be doing. Lance and I can handle this."

Hennessey shook his head. "This. *This* is what an agent does, and he doesn't take a break because it's hard. We don't stop until we catch the guy, and don't let anyone tell you otherwise."

A shiver climbed up my spine. I felt a ghost again, but this time it was Hennessey, mentoring me, preparing me for a time he wouldn't be around to call the shots. What would finally kill him? A heart attack from greasy diner food? Or would it be Laguardia? Not if I could help it.

"Be careful, okay?" The words slipped out before I could stop them.

His expression softened, but I never heard what he was going to say. Some bit of male bravado, probably. They hadn't gotten him for this long, so he clearly knew how to take care of himself. But then I remembered the burger and milkshake and thought maybe he really didn't.

Like Peter Pan, he could fight and put on a good

front, but he was just a boy at heart, never quite grown up. And who did that make me? Wendy Darling, thrust into a world she was unsuited for, in constant need of saving.

Ugh.

Hennessey stayed true to his attitude of inclusion by having me tag along to the briefing with Brody. I followed him in silence and made myself unobtrusive while Hennessey filled him in. I had no wish to steal any of the glory, however small it may be at this point. We had narrowed down the pool to three possible locations. Once we received more information about the owner-ship, we would narrow it down and initiate surveillance on the possible buildings. All this Hennessey said in clear, concise language that would easily translate into a report Brody would write for the upper levels.

Brody grunted his approval as he jotted notes. He turned a piercing gaze on me. "How are you finding the work?"

At turns exhilarating and boring, meaningful and empty. "It's going very well, sir. I'm coming up to speed quickly."

He nodded, though his eyes remained considering.

Hennessey cleared his throat. "I'd like to take this opportunity to request a change in assignment. I think a different partner would be better suited to this case, one with more experience."

All the breath left me. Completely silent, I fell apart in that office chair. He wanted to get rid of me? I hadn't been impressive, okay. But to request reassignment after five days of working together? God. And he hadn't even given me a heads up before we came in here.

Brody glanced at me idly, seeming to find amusement in my shock. Bastard.

He turned to Hennessey. "You know you're going to have to provide a better reason than that if you want management to sign off on this."

"You have final say," Hennessey said.

Brody nodded, conceding. "Fine. You'll have to do better if you want *me* to sign off on it."

"She attracted the attention of Fuentes. He'll get word back to Carlos that there's a rookie on his case. It's unusual for such a high profile fugitive. He'll take an interest."

"And that would be bad," Brody said. A statement, not a question.

"Yes, that would be bad," Hennessey repeated, a touch of mockery in his tone. "We want him thinking he has this wrapped up. We don't want him changing the schedule around or doubling up on security."

Brody shrugged. "If he finds out we have a rookie working his case, he isn't likely to beef up security, is he?"

Hennessey's expression was bored. "He'll know something is up. Don't make the mistake of underestimating him this close to the finish line."

New shock flooded my veins. Was he trying to get himself on Brody's shit list? First he'd sprung this on me, now he was reprimanding Brody? Brody may not have the power to fire him, but he wasn't a fun guy to piss off.

Brody's eyebrows lowered. "It's my call who's on the case, and I say it's Holmes. You got a problem with that, you come back with something substantial."

Hennessey nodded, seeming unsurprised. "Understood."

"Dismissed, gentlemen." Brody paused. "And lady."

I managed not to roll my eyes. Law enforcement officers were the least politically correct people you'd ever meet, but I was too pissed off to find the dichotomy amusing. I pushed through the door and let it swing back in Hennessey's face. Fuck him. Just fuck him and his request for a new partner.

"Rookie," he called, and that made me angrier.

Fuck the fake endearment too.

I sped up. The thin office carpeting blurred beneath my feet, as if I were watching a runway before takeoff. I wished I could really fly away and never have to face the man coming after me. He didn't want me? Fine. But I hated that he'd hurt me. When had I given another person that power? Never. Not ever. Not even my father had hurt me. It hadn't hurt, not even when he…

"Holmes. Agent Holmes," Hennessey spoke lower, having caught up to me now, but fuck his bogus respect, the sudden desire for privacy. Where was his conspiratorial murmur before that meeting? Blindsided. I'd been blindsided. Now I was shaking and cold and hating that he could affect me.

What do you remember?

No one had ever hurt me.

"Samantha," he said, out of breath. "Sam!" Frustration roughened his voice. It would have pleased me, if it hadn't also been laced with regret. Fine. If we were going to do this, we'd do it in private. We'd have to work together, at least until he found something more "substantial" with which to get rid of me. And I'd learned years ago to face my problems head on.

I turned to him, and the expression on his face sliced through me like a gust of cold wind. I couldn't even place what I saw there. Guilt? Concern? I had to scroll through B-movie reels and strange flickering dreams, because for sure no man had ever looked at me that way, not in real life.

He led me into a supply closet, and I let him. I felt numb. Cold. *Are you afraid?* No. I couldn't feel a thing.

"Jesus." Hennessey rubbed my hands between his in the dark. "Samantha. I'm sorry."

Stop being a rookie, I told myself derisively. But I *was* a rookie. I was a kid, almost. A little girl, deep inside.

"Why didn't you tell me?" I asked.

"I couldn't." His voice roughened with guilt. "He's not telling us something. It might be important. I had to see if he'd give us a clue."

I stared at him in shock. "What?" I asked stupidly.

He grimaced, as if he didn't want to explain. "Your position on the case, as one of the leads. It had to seem strange to you. Unexpected."

"Yes." *Unusual.* That was the word Hennessey had used in Brody's office.

"I don't know why he assigned you to the case, but I don't like it."

I stiffened. "Yeah, I got that much, thanks."

"No. Not because I don't want you for a partner. You're...also unexpected. More than I expected. But if something else is going on here, we need to know about it. I had to spring it on you so you'd be surprised too."

Jesus. It had been a ruse to get information, like the threats he made to Fuentes. To me. If I believed him. And I wanted to believe him. In the aftermath, those threats made sense. Lying to an inmate was a tried and true interrogation technique. But in the moment they'd felt so damn real. As was the relief I felt now. Had I cared that much what Hennessey thought of me? I'd only known him a week, which was nothing. I didn't care.

A lie.

So I had a little a crush on my partner. No big deal. It didn't mean anything. Just pheromones and adrenalin. A chemical reaction. It didn't have to mean anything.

I nodded slowly. "Yeah. Okay."

"Are you sure?" His eyes scanned mine. "You looked ready to bite my head off out there."

My breath left in a long, stabilizing rush. "It took me by surprise. I wish you'd have warned me."

"Sorry. I wasn't sure if you'd give us away."

"I wouldn't have. We're partners." I raised my eyebrows. "You have to trust me, or I'll be the one putting in a request for a new partner."

He nodded. "Fair enough."

"Well, *did* he give us a clue? My head was busy exploding, so I didn't hear."

His lips twisted—derisive, but more at himself. "I'm not sure. *He'll take an interest*, I said, and it didn't sound like Brody was surprised by that. It didn't sound like he'd mind."

"What does it mean?" I hated that I didn't already know.

"It means he's running his own op. One we don't know about."

"That's bullshit," I said, and I meant it. Even a rookie knew that was dangerous. Not for Laguardia, necessarily. Dangerous to *us*, the agents on the case.

Hennessey nodded grimly. "Unfortunately, it's not uncommon. Everything's need-to-know."

An image flickered through my mind: Hennessey, stumbling through the dark. Caught and tortured. "Well, tell him we fucking need to know."

The corner of his lip tilted up. "That's the first time I've heard you swear, rookie."

Every time he said the word *rookie* it got a little softer. A little sweeter. I told myself I was imagining it...but I wasn't. Was the chemical reaction happening on both sides? It didn't have to mean anything. His eyes were warmer than I'd ever seen them, a deep gray, like liquid mercury in the shadows of the dimly-lit room. He felt it too.

"What happens now?" I asked, almost daring him to comment on this growing attraction between us. *With the case*, I amended silently. But even I didn't believe that.

Girlish crushes were swift attacking and venomous, wrapping their muscled bodies around me and squeezing tight. It happened from time to time. My film teacher in the senior year of high school. My lab instructor in Chem 201. The head of admissions at Quantico. Always an older handsome man in a position of authority.

Daddy issues. That was what the psychology textbook never said.

"We're close," he said. "Three places that match Fuentes's description, a secluded location, and easy access to the water. Once we get more intel about the ownership, we'll narrow it down even further. Then the real fun begins."

I raised an eyebrow. "And then we catch a criminal."

"Then we stop a massive shipment of drugs before they hit the streets. As for catching Laguardia, I appreciate the vote of confidence, but even I probably won't close a case this big in three weeks." He paused. "But you should know this. I don't intend to catch him. I intend to kill him."

My eyes widened. Most people would agree with such a statement, in their hearts if not out loud. It violated both law and ethics, and yet I couldn't deny that the world would be a safer place without Carlos in it. Executed. Without due process.

It would be murder.

"I'm on your side," I said slowly. I meant as his partner, even in this dark goal of his. I meant something deeper too, more elemental, but I could hardly admit that to him, much less myself.

His head cocked, as if he were analyzing me. His brow furrowed, marking vague curiosity about the girl who'd thrown her hat in his ring. It became an offering I'd made him, and I waited with bated breath for him to accept. He might not really want me on his side. In some ways he'd been pushing me away from the first day I'd landed on his case. In other ways, I sensed he needed something only I could provide. It wasn't hubris. I had a fresh perspective and enthusiasm. But more than that, I had shadows inside me. He might not know where they came from, but he could see them.

The heat in his eyes changed. No longer professional intensity, something else burned there. Something inappropriate but welcome all the same. My lids lowered in invitation as I stared at the passion in his eyes, the dark steel ringed with black. I waited for him to do what his expression promised, and he didn't let me down.

His head bent, and his lips captured mine. The kiss was sudden and shocking—the culmination of every taut moment between us. Inevitable. His mouth moved over mine, his tongue moved inside me, speaking more eloquently than his words could. *Trust me,* they said. And mine answered, *I already do. I can't help it, I do.*

Give yourself to me, they said. And mine answered,

I'm already yours. Can't you feel it too?

A startled sound came from his throat, and I drank it down, pleased to have caused it.

He pulled back finally, panting slightly. "I think you're more dangerous than you let on, rookie."

My chest grew tight. He was right. *He knew.*

Dangerous. What a tripwire word. After all, how many people had caught a serial killer at age ten? A truly innocent child wouldn't even have known what all that blood meant. Wouldn't have known what he was doing to the children before he killed them. So how had I been so sure? No one had ever hurt me.

With my stomach in a knot, I pushed out of the dark room and sucked in a deep breath of stale office air. I crossed the hallway quickly, not looking back. The soft sound of his footfalls followed me.

"Samantha?" He stood behind me, his breath warm where it ruffled the hair at my temple.

I said nothing.

"Are you upset that I kissed you?"

Still nothing. I couldn't have spoken. Upset? Yes, I was upset. And I wanted him to kiss me again.

Finally he sighed and asked, "What do you see?"

Only then did I realize where I'd stopped. At the whiteboard with all the core case information pinned up. Maps and lists and one black-and-white grainy photograph.

The man in the photograph looked directly at the camera. He knew where the cameras were located. He also knew the footage quality was poor enough to make it irrelevant. What was he feeling in that moment? Defiance? Or incipient curiosity to know who was hunting him, a restless desire to meet their mechanical gaze?

It felt strange to humanize him, a man who had committed such atrocities, but despite what Hennessey had said about the scope of our jobs, it felt strange to think of him as just another criminal. He wasn't just another criminal. He was scarier than the rest of them, more powerful. Smarter, too. Yes, I had a healthy dose of respect for this man I reviled. *Daddy issues.*

"He's always cold," I answered without turning.

"How do you know?" A question he had asked before and asked again. People would think I was crazy if I kept pushing this point, and maybe that was why I did it.

"He's wearing a thick jacket. A hat. I think that's a scarf tucked into his collar. And look at those heavy boots."

"Well, maybe it's cold outside."

"No. Look at the other people. Jeans and a T-shirt. That girl is wearing flip-flops." Innocent people with no idea who stood in their midst. "And it was sixty-five degrees at that location on the date and time this still frame was taken. Brisk, but not enough for all those layers."

Hennessey was silent a moment. Conceding my point, I thought. "Why does it matter?" he asked finally.

I shook my head, finally turning to face him. I had

no answer for that. It shouldn't matter, but it did. Laguardia was one of the most powerful men in existence. He could build empires and topple governments. He was a fucking machine. But he had a flaw, and that made him human. It made him catchable. And I was going to catch him.

CHAPTER FIVE

BY THE END of the week, my neck was sore, my back was stiff, and my body hummed with a kind of expectant energy. I filled the bathtub with steaming water and threw in a ball of moisturizing bath fizz. The scent of lavender filled the small room, riding on the steam. A thin film of condensation formed on the bathroom mirror, turning my naked body hazy and blurred. I was prettier this way, I thought. Surface only, out of focus. Drunk college guys had certainly thought so, but then they probably said that to any girl.

I stepped into the bath and let the hot water wash away all my tension. I'd never understood the appeal of hooking up, but I'd done it. Anything to be normal, to *pretend* to be normal. So I'd hit the clubs with some friends and find a random guy to disappoint me twice before morning. Get dressed. Walk away. Forget his name. Had I even asked for it? Whatever. Typical college student. Things were a little trickier as an adult. Now guys wanted to date. They were thinking about commitment, about starting a family.

No, thank you.

Now it was the older guys who wanted a quick fuck.

Men like Hennessey. Most likely divorced and career-focused, they didn't want a goddamned commitment. They wanted a screw in the supply closet. Except he hadn't wanted to fuck. He'd wanted to talk, so what did that mean?

Men were confusing.

I spread my legs in the warm bath. Closing my eyes, I let my head fall back against the porcelain. My sex was already slippery from the soap. Cold gunmetal eyes. A sardonic smile. The word *rookie* used like an endearment. I rubbed myself quickly, roughly, being as hard on my body as I wished he would be. *I want him to hurt me.* With that strange thought, I came in tight pulses that sent ripples through the bath water.

I breathed the hot, humid air in the aftermath. What did it mean? Nothing. I laughed under my breath. It meant I was horny. Nothing more.

After drying myself, I pulled on a tank top from a music festival and loose sultan pants, and I settled down to paint my nails. It was a luxury, a brief nod to my femininity in a career path dominated by men.

My style was eclectic and excessively feminine—frilly and glittered when plain would have sufficed. I tried to tone it back for the office for obvious reasons. Partly because any extra accessories, like earrings, could be used against me by a perp in the unlikely event of a foot chase. The other reason was because I tried my hardest to paint the picture of a driven professional. Of a severe law enforcement officer.

Even my nails were filed short and painted with a clear coat for strength. The only exception was my toenails, which I shaped and painted in a full self-service pedicure every week. Sometimes I used a deep red, others a girlish pink. Today I chose a light blue, drawing from some deep desire for open sky. It was as if I bundled all my vanity into my feet, which I'd stuff away into sensible low-heeled shoes for work each day.

I was waiting for my toenails to finish drying when the doorbell rang. I glanced at the clock. Ten on a Friday night. I wasn't expecting anyone, but despite being a woman, alone, I wasn't afraid. I could kick the asses of most perps. More importantly, I'd learned long ago that criminals didn't knock at the front door. They lured you into white vans. They lived in your own home.

The image through the peephole made me smile. I schooled my expression and opened the door.

Hennessey stood on the step, looking casual and right at home. The faded black fabric of his T-shirt matched his eyes. It molded to the lean muscles on his chest, revealing what the suits had left hidden. Strength. Power. Sexiness. Faded jeans and a well-worn T-shirt was practically a wardrobe of seduction on a man like this, the masculine equivalent of showing up in nothing but a trench coat and high heels.

If you want me, take me. My body responded like a live wire, primed from spending the whole week working with him and having lost its professional inhibitions through exhaustion. I could spin these fantasies in my head, and no one would ever know.

Especially him.

I may have crushed on older men, I may have fucked them, but I resented them too. I resented their allure and their dominance even as I craved them. Part and parcel of the daddy issues, I supposed.

"What are you doing here?" I asked, a little brusquely.

"We found the warehouse. It's owned by a subsidiary of Laguardia." He held up a stack of stuffed file folders. "I've got shipment routes going to and from that dock. We can narrow down which one it is based on pay loads and time of day."

"Okay, let me rephrase. How did you find *me*?"

He raised an eyebrow. "FBI Agent."

"Stalker."

He lifted the case of beer he held in his other hand. "I come bearing gifts."

I sighed and stood back to let him in. "Forgiven."

He passed me by, his gaze roving down my body. The tank top barely concealed my breasts or my nipples, which had hardened in the night air. A sliver of my belly and the upper curves of my hips were revealed by the low-slung pants. And at my feet, the sky blue stood out like some sort of testament to my youth, a sharp contrast to the hardened, experienced, jaded man in front of me.

He froze when he looked down. Something ran through his body, a subtle tension I could barely discern and couldn't define. He shook his head briefly, as if to clear it. Then he continued inside, and I might have imagined it, except for the sensual awareness awakened in my own body.

He had seen me as a woman and wanted me. That wasn't the surprising part. A moderately pretty girl, young and friendly, I could find interested men by walking into the nearest bar. They wanted to fuck me and leave me, though I never gave them the chance. Even if I did consent to fuck them, just to see if this time, *this time*, it would be different, I was always the one who left first.

No, it wasn't surprising that he wanted me. The truly surprising part was that I wanted him right back. Wanted his body, his attention.

And strangely, wanted him to stay.

I led him to the table in the kitchen, a piece made of reclaimed wood I'd found on a weekend trip to the coast. The top was a slab of thick slats that used to be a fence. The legs were connected with old brass door hinges. The man at the farmer's market expected me to haggle, but the table was worth far more than I paid for it. It gave me a kind of contentedness every time I saw it.

We spent the night combing the files, drinking his beer and ordering a pizza to help us through. Sometimes when he looked at me, it seemed like...well, but he never acted on it. There was no touching or anything too inappropriate at all, just two agents working a case together.

Colleagues, yes.

Friends, maybe. Friends who kissed.

But lovers? The official Bureau regulations would bar such a thing. I couldn't let personal feelings get in the way of catching Laguardia, and I doubted Hennessey made such allowances either. He hadn't gotten to be a renowned agent by getting distracted by prettily painted toes.

Although, he had shown up at my place, instead of calling me into the office. Instead of waiting until morning. So maybe he was a little interested. And judging from the way he kept glancing at my body, a little distracted too.

Hours passed going through pages and pretending not to notice how close he was to me. The hour hand crossed the midnight Rubicon and continued into the early hours of morning. My eyelids drooped, blurring the words in front of me. Both of us were moving slower and talking less. We were falling asleep, neither of us willing to end this tenuous peace.

A ringing sound startled me, and I dropped the pen I was holding. His cell phone.

He sent me an apologetic glance. "I've got to take this."

"You can use the living room," I offered, for privacy.

I could still hear him when he answered brusquely and spoke in low tones, but I couldn't make out his words. Just as well, because my mind was mush at this point. Maybe I'd rest my eyes so I could be alert and ready to work when he was done with his call.

The steady murmur of his voice was my lullaby, a gentle shove from the shores of consciousness. I drifted away, barely aware of the papers pinned under my cheek. Barely aware of the gentle caress of my temple, brushing my hair from my face. Barely aware of the strong arms lifting me.

He shushed my mumbled protest, carrying me to my bedroom. The sheets were cool along my body. Too cold. I wanted him to join me, but by the time I reached for him, by the time I opened my eyes, he was already gone.

✦   ✦   ✦

ON SATURDAY MORNING, we met in the office. He shared a secret sleepy smile with me before speaking to the group of agents he'd called in to work the weekend. We knew which warehouse Carlos would be using, and we had three possible dates for the shipment.

The first window was only four days away. We already had surveillance on the location so we could watch guard activity and learn their security protocols. With painstaking timing and coordination, we established a plan to bypass the outer perimeter and then confront each inner level until all opposing forces were subdued. That was the hard part.

We'd find out then if Laguardia was among them. Only after would we know if we'd caught our prey. We didn't have anything as precise as a harpoon. We had a net that would scoop out fish and debris and a hundred other things—and hopefully the shark as well.

Hennessey headed joint task force meetings with the DEA and the local police. Together, we planned the operation with cunning and expertise, and the entire time, I waited for Brody to tell me there'd been a mistake. I wasn't meant to be part of something this big, this important. I waited for Hennessey to ask Brody for another partner, and for real this time. He'd be better off with someone more experienced than me, wouldn't he?

But neither of those things happened. Someone else served up the cold reminder of how poorly suited I was for the job. Lance.

"You seem tense," he mumbled when I'd fallen back in my chair on a rare break in my cubicle. Hennessey had disappeared for some meeting with the bigwigs, so for the umpteenth time, I was left to go over the plans by myself.

I shrugged. "It's a big deal."

"For the Bureau or for your career?"

The venom in Lance's voice shocked me. I sat forward slowly, focusing on him. "For both. Is that a problem?"

He shook his head and disappeared behind the cloth divider, but I wouldn't be that easily put off. For months, he had been my only friend here. And now, was he turning his back on me? Or had I turned my back on him?

I hadn't meant to abandon him when I got this assignment. I'd been busy as hell, and Lance had been working in the same conference room for most of the time. But we didn't have the private talks over the cubicle walls anymore. And if Lance were a little jealous of me getting to do fieldwork, it would only be natural. After all, he'd started here before me.

So why had I gotten the assignment?

I shook the thought away and focused on the problem at hand. Namely, Lance, resolutely staring at his desk as if it held the answers to the universe instead of his timesheet.

"Hey," I said softly. "I need your help with something, if you're up for it."

He tilted his head without looking at me. "Help with what?"

"It's for the case. But Hennessey wouldn't approve." That got his attention. "He might be mad, actually. So you can't tell him. It's okay if you don't want to do it."

When he turned, he had a faint smile. "Let's go. You can fill me in on the way."

"You sure you aren't worried about Hennessey?"

A snort. "He can kiss my ass."

Definitely jealous.

Though it occurred to me for the first time that maybe he wasn't only jealous of my assignment. The quiet talks, the lunches spent together, the casual invitations to a weekend movie if I didn't have anything else to do. If I wasn't mistaken, Lance had a crush on me.

Shit. I hadn't realized it, because I never thought of him that way. It was fine, I supposed, as long as he knew nothing would come of it. Not on this field trip, certainly. Not ever. I suspected he'd come along to piss off Hennessey more than anything. That was fine too. A little professional competition never hurt anybody.

The raid was tomorrow night. We had planned it down to the minute. Since tomorrow would be a long, exhausting day, we'd all been dismissed early. *Go home, get some sleep.* Officially the goal was to make sure the agents were well-rested for a raid, not edging toward exhaustion. Unofficially, a grim undertone reminded us that everyone might not make it through.

We maintained every safety protocol from full shields to tight formations on entry, but these situations were always chaotic. Or so I had heard. This would be my first raid.

And hopefully not my last.

CHAPTER SIX

A WOMAN KNELT over a flower bed as Lance pulled us up to the curb. The brakes squeaked, and she looked up, raising a gloved hand to shield her eyes from the sun. A slatted straw hat obscured her face, but I got the impression of a slender, graceful form. I stepped out of the car, and Lance did the same, both of us careful to shut our doors softly, the noise barely disturbing the soothing strains of a large wind chime. The white wraparound porch presented a picturesque view of domestic tranquility.

So this was Carlos's prostitute. Or was she his mistress? Girlfriend? None of the words seemed to fit her. She was pretty in an understated way, not at all the sort of woman I'd imagined consorting with a major criminal. But then, looks could be deceiving. I was a testament to that. She and I both had a petite frame and pale, milky skin that contrasted sharply with thick brown locks. It made men think we were innocent. In both cases, apparently, they were wrong.

The screen door twanged, and a man appeared. Before we could reach Mia Palermo, he stood in front of her. This was in the files too. Her husband. A former

FBI agent. Did he know what she'd done? Who she'd done it with? He must have. And yet here he was, standing in front of her, protecting her from unexpected FBI agents. I knew that stance with innate recognition. He'd do anything to keep her safe; he'd take a bullet for her. It was love.

"Ms. Palermo," Lance began.

"Martinez," the man corrected, none too kindly. "You can address her as Mrs. Martinez, if I let you address her at all."

Lance raised an eyebrow. I could tell he was annoyed at the man's brusque tone, but making the guy mad would get us nowhere.

"Mr. Martinez," I said. "If you could spare a minute of your time. We're from the local branch—"

"I know where you're from. I could smell you a mile away. What I don't know is why you're bothering me."

Bothering *her*, he meant. His broad shoulders almost blocked her from view. My heart clenched at the show of protectiveness, of possession. What would it feel like to have someone love you like that? To have them know all your worst secrets and want you anyway?

"We're working the Laguardia case, sir, and it's vital that we speak with Mrs. Martinez regarding any information she may have on the matter," Lance said.

I stared at him, a bit surprised that he'd be so insistent when he was so laid back in the office. Then again, this was probably his first piece of fieldwork, even if it wasn't strictly sanctioned. It made sense he'd want to make the most of it.

"She's already given a statement," Martinez said curtly. "Several."

"The pages on her are mostly blacked out," I murmured.

Martinez raised an eyebrow, his piercing gaze falling on me. "Then you don't have high enough clearance. So I have to ask again, why are you here?"

I decided to answer honestly. "If things go well, we're going to confront him soon. I'd like to know what we're up against, so my partner and I don't get killed when we do."

Martinez's gaze switched back to Lance. He looked him down and then up again, clearly unimpressed. Between the two of us, we weren't an extremely imposing team. But then, Lance wasn't really my partner. Hennessey was.

And he's going to be pissed.

Damn, I wished I weren't going behind his back like this. I still felt a niggling resentment that he'd turned on me in Brody's office, that he hadn't given me a heads up if he'd been planning to ferret out information. But it didn't make sense to berate him for that if I wouldn't give him the same level of trust.

Martinez sighed, and I could see we'd won him over. Maybe it helped that we were such a ragtag team. We clearly needed all the help we could get.

"Ten minutes," Martinez said. "So ask the important questions first, because I'm cutting you off a second longer."

The woman, Mia Martinez, peeked around the man's shoulder, an amused expression on her face. "Now that you've negotiated for my time, could I make one small request?"

Something flickered in Martinez's face at her words. *Negotiated for my time* could have a different, darker meaning in Laguardia's circles. Had she been pimped out? Passed around? If so, it would make sense she'd be sensitive to things being decided for her. But if Martinez regretted his heavy-handedness, he didn't show it. He'd do anything to keep her safe, I realized, even hurt her.

Martinez murmured for her ears only, but I still heard him say, "You don't have to talk to them at all, if you don't want to. I can send them away."

"No," she said. "I want to. They should know what they're going to be facing. But…only the girl. Okay?"

"Done," Martinez said.

She sent Lance an apologetic look. "I'm sorry. It's nothing personal, just that—"

Lance cleared his throat. The tips of his ears turned pink. "You don't have to explain, Mrs. Martinez. Our goal as agents is to make you comfortable."

Right out of the student handbook, kids.

Mia led me to a picnic table in their backyard. We left the men up front for what I imagined included a lot of glaring and posturing. In the shade, I got a better look at Mia. She was younger than I'd expected. I pictured the file…she would be twenty-eight, with wide eyes and porcelain skin that hinted at twenty.

But her eyes told a different story. She could have been ancient for all the weary knowledge in her eyes. It was a strange juxtaposition, one I recognized from Hennessey. I wondered how much they had in common. Another pang of guilt hit me. He should be here with me, interviewing her right now. He would know the right questions. Unlike me.

"Mrs. Martinez," I began.

"Mia," she corrected. "Please. I'm not so formal among friends."

She was putting me at ease, and it worked. A slight blush heated my cheeks. She was really far too subtle for a guy like Laguardia, except she'd stayed with him for so many years. And then I knew what to ask.

"How did you meet Laguardia?"

She slanted me a look, as if trying to gauge my sincerity. I kept my expression still and open, because I *was* sincere. Unlike Hennessey, I wanted to understand the man behind the proverbial *Wanted* poster.

"He picked me up off the street," she said finally. "I was young. Too young. He gave me food, clothing. Medical attention. Education. I would have died out there, starved or been beaten to death by a guy three times my age. But he took me in."

He sounded like a saint. But we both knew better. "And he had sex with you."

She nodded, unsurprised at the dark turn of the conversation. "He had sex with me. At the time, it seemed fair enough. Like payment. Nothing is free on the streets."

"You said *at the time.* How do you see it now?"

"I'm not sure…" Her lips pressed together. "You'll probably think I'm romanticizing it, and maybe I am, but I felt like we understood each other. It's not easy, in that life, to open yourself up to someone, to become vulnerable. Even sex isn't always intimate."

"But between you it was?" I couldn't hide the doubt from my voice.

"Between us, everything was intimate. And nothing was. I'm sorry I can't explain it better. I recognized the same darkness in him as I had in myself." She paused, twirling a leaf on the knotted wood table. "Did you know my father sexually abused me?"

The question flashed through me, a painful burst of light in the dark, even though I'd known that already. It was hard to imagine that on top of whatever abuse she'd suffered with Carlos. It changed a person, to look evil in the face at so young an age. I should know. But maybe they weren't so different, flipsides of the same coin. The criminal and the victim. The aggressor and the defenseless. One couldn't exist without the other.

"I'm sorry," I murmured.

"We had that in common."

Surprise lifted my eyebrows. "You mean Carlos? He was abused?"

A nod. "You know, I'm not saying that as an excuse, either for him or for me. We made our choices. But it leaves its mark on you, even when you think you're over it. I don't think he would have been capable of a regular relationship."

I couldn't help but ask, softly, "And you?"

Her lips twisted in a wry smile. "I wouldn't call my relationship with Tyler conventional. And I still have problems, being…what's the word? Fatalistic. That's what Tyler says. I get sort of detached, go through the motions. It drives him crazy, because he wants me to be present, you know? But we work on it together in counseling."

I tried to imagine the gruff, uncompromising Martinez in a therapy session and failed. But he must have a softer side he showed Mia. That part I could imagine. She had a quiet, nonjudgmental way about her, as if I could tell her anything and she wouldn't be shocked. And she wouldn't reject me either. It was seductive in a way that cleavage and hooker boots could never compete with. Carlos Laguardia had more discerning taste than I'd have expected.

She leaned forward. "I'm telling you all this because if you're going after Laguardia, you have to understand he's like a dog who's been kicked too many times before. If you get close, he's going to lash out at you."

"I see," I murmured as an uncomfortable realization settled over me. Laguardia would have every reason to lash out at us. We *were* going to kick him, figuratively. Literally too, if Hennessey was serious about wanting Laguardia dead.

I remembered watching *Lady and the Tramp* as a kid, where the dogs ate spaghetti by candlelight and viewed the pound as a jail. There was something chilling in the realization that I was the dogcatcher in this scenario. I was one of the good guys, but only depending on the story. Told from another perspective, I was the villain.

Her eyes grew distant, as if she looked into the past. "The thing about Carlos is that he doesn't mean well. Whenever possible, he would try to do the wrong thing, the cruel thing. It became a point of pride for him. And then…well, it tore him up inside. It split him into the man and this other type of being. Like an animal, but smarter, more cunning."

"Dr. Jekyll and Mr. Hyde."

She cocked her head. "Who?"

A flush heated my cheeks. I felt stupid, as if I'd been trying to talk down to her. I knew that she'd dropped out the first year of high school, that she'd run away to escape her father's abuse. And ran into Carlos instead. She didn't seem to regret it. Instead, she seemed oddly loyal to him, protective as she warned me away.

Her expression was guileless and curious.

"It's a play," I said. "There was this doctor who wanted to find a way to remove the evil parts of man. He experimented on himself, but all he ended up doing was splitting himself into two parts. The good man and the evil one."

"He can't be both anymore. One or the other." A mournful glint entered her eyes. I suspected this was a play she had witnessed not on the stage, but in real life.

I nodded.

"And how did it end?"

"The good doctor grew more and more unstable." In fact, there was a female character, a prostitute. It felt a little pointed, as if it were about *her*. And by the end, the evil Mr. Hyde had killed her. In his grief and to protect all others, Dr. Jekyll killed himself. These types of stories often ended in death. I cleared my throat, thinking of a lie. "Then he came up with another potion to put himself back together again."

That wasn't really the way it ended, and Mia smiled sadly. She wasn't fooled. She might look sweet and innocent, almost perpetually childlike, but she had seen the worst side of humanity. She'd lived among the Mr. Hydes of the world and somehow escaped to this domestic idyll.

I stared at her with a growing sense of surrealism. We looked alike. Dark hair that shone in the light. Porcelain skin. The similarities ran deeper than that. We both had crazy, fucked up fathers. Only, mine had hurt other children. Hers had hurt *her*, so looking at her was like an alternate reality version of myself. This was what I'd be if things had been different.

She was beautiful, with an air of contentedness, so it wasn't a bad option, really. Except things hadn't always been good for her. Bad things had happened in her past, with her father, on the streets, with Carlos, and I knew that from reading more than her file. All those blacked out lines, those top-secret words. And the past she couldn't quite forget.

Her eyes held shadows. Hollows in her eyes, empty spaces carved out from moments I could only guess at. Emotional scar tissue, and no amount of her husband's love or protection could ever erase it completely.

CHAPTER SEVEN

B Y THE TIME Mia and I returned to the front of the house, Lance was conversing seriously with Tyler Martinez. About Carlos, probably. It hadn't really occurred to me that the ex-agent could have as much valuable insight as Carlos's former girlfriend. That was smart of Lance. Capable, too, that he'd swayed someone initially hostile to talk to him.

"Did he tell you anything?" I asked on the ride back, looking at his side profile.

He shifted gears as the light turned green. "Not anything we can use. He warned me away. Said Carlos would do things on his own terms. Always has, always will."

"That's about what Mia said," I admitted.

Depressing advice from two people who had been steamrolled by Carlos once upon time. And they'd managed to escape and build new lives for themselves, so they knew what they were talking about.

If I were smart, I'd take their advice. I'd back off Carlos and find some smaller fish to fry. But this was my assignment, my career. This was my *purpose*, and I couldn't leave it alone any sooner than Carlos could stop being a criminal. We were at cross purposes, he and I. One of us had to lose, and even knowing it would be me, I couldn't stop trying.

Lance was quiet for the rest of the drive, a thoughtful look on his face. He was young. Around the same age as me, but he *felt* young. He looked it, too, with angular features almost too big for his face and hair that tended to flop in his eyes by the end of the day. His body was gangly, though strong.

I could see the building blocks of a handsome, well-built man, but he wasn't fully formed yet. He needed more bulk and he needed more experience—at least, for my tastes. I'd always been attracted to older men. Even knowing it was due to daddy issues didn't diminish it. The body wants what it wants. And the heart yearns for acceptance, something Lance's innocence could never really provide.

His mouth opened as if he wanted to say something, but he shook his head. "Just keep your eyes open."

My eyebrows rose. "Okay...that sounds like a threat."

He grimaced slightly. "I don't think it's a coincidence you're on this case."

First Hennessey, now Lance. I was surrounded by conspiracy theorists. But that didn't mean they were wrong.

I bit my lip, thinking. "Did Martinez say something about it?"

A pause. "He said you could be sisters. You and Mia,

when you were coming back around the house. That you looked alike."

Jesus. There were a hundred reasons I was on this case. No, there was only one reason.

If only I had someone to confide in. I wanted to spill my darkest secrets without facing condemnation. I needed to lay out all the pieces and have someone talk me through it. I had to believe the jagged pieces fit together, if I knew the proper order.

My thoughts went to Hennessey. Could I trust him? At the very least, I should tell him about this visit to Mia. Then if he didn't flip out…if we continued talking…no, I couldn't trust him. That course had been set a long time ago. It hadn't even been my decision.

When Lance pulled his car to a stop, I got out and murmured a quick goodbye. He waited until I got in my car before leaving the parking garage himself. We were both supposed to head home, along with the rest of the team. Relax, recharge. Be in top shape for the bust tomorrow.

So why was Hennessey's dark sedan in the space next to mine?

Without thinking too much about my decision, I got out of my car and used my badge to enter the building after hours. The atrium was a large space with sleek glass walls. Etched into the marble floor were the scales of justice, ominous and weighty. Exhausted-looking agents headed for the exit, blindly crossing the scales of justice, trampling them. The building was never really empty, and there was always something going down on one case or another.

I had to pass my cubicle, and Lance's, on the way. They both sat empty, of course. Unimpressive spaces for the rookies. Really, no part of the building looked glamorous or shiny the way they did in the movies. We were more about budget restrictions and safety protocols.

At least, we had been, until Hennessey had arrived with his high profile case and planned tactical maneuvers. He was the closest I'd ever seen to the romantic ideal of a law enforcement officer, all honor and intelligence. But even though I believed in him, I wondered if there was a dark side. How far would he go to see Carlos behind bars? Would he shoot first and ask questions later? Would I?

The sparse temporary office Hennessey had been using was empty, but the light was on, indicating he hadn't left for the day. The sound of voices lured me farther down the hall, toward Brody's office. As I got closer, I could hear the menace underlying both masculine voices. A thread of worry wound its way through my body, touching off a rapid heartbeat. This building saw its share of bravado and male posturing, but this was sharper.

I stood in front of the door. Someone spoke angrily, in a burst I couldn't comprehend. The other person responded something about a fire, and going down in flames—though whether that was a hypothetical inferno, I didn't know.

I knocked. The voices quieted.

Brody's voice. "Come in."

Pressing inside, I saw Hennessey standing by the window, looking out. Even in the small office, he'd found the place with a view. The tense lines of his body spoke of his frustration. Brody also had a pissed off expression, but then that was pretty much normal. He wore his cynicism like a second skin. I had only ever seen him earnest once before.

"Sorry," I said, apologizing for the intrusion. Even though I'd done it on purpose. If it was about the case, I had a right to know. And if it was about me…well, I should know that too. "Is there something I can help with?"

"Yes." Brody nodded. "We've received intel that the drop is going to be made tonight. We're going to have to move quickly to catch them."

From the side of the office, Hennessey made a hiss of frustration. "And work blind, since we don't have time to get the snipers in place."

"We have good men. Sorry," Brody added to me. "And women."

Hennessey shook his head, his displeasure evident in the hard set of his face, the metallic fire in his eyes. "If we can even get all of them in. If they answer their cell phones and get their asses into the office in the next hour. If they haven't been drinking or a hundred other things that could keep them from being alert."

Brody's eyes darkened. "I'm sure you'll adjust the

plan accordingly. You *are* the lead of this operation."

Hennessey snorted in derision. "Right, which means you override the most important decision. And if I step down, you'll do it anyway, and the whole thing will be a clusterfuck."

"It's your decision," Brody said placidly.

Hennessey pointed at him. "If we lose an agent, this is on your head."

"Don't lose sight of the objective, Hennessey." Brody's eyes glittered. "We're here to nail Carlos to the wall, and how are you going to do that if he comes and goes before you're even in position? He's moving now, so you move now."

Hennessey stared at him coldly, and I held my breath. I half expected him to tell Brody to go fuck himself. At least then he wouldn't have the professional responsibility of said clusterfuck. But finally he gave a short nod and headed into the hallway.

I stood to follow him, but Brody cleared his throat. My eyebrow rose. An unspoken challenge filled the room as I waited for my boss to speak. As I waited for him to give himself away.

He paused, as if deciding how much to say. "It's important we move on this guy now. Now, before he goes underground."

Curiosity pierced my frustration. "Sir?"

Leaning forward, he spoke lower. "What I said before, about the unrest within his organization, it's getting worse. And fast. They're either dying or disappearing, like rats running for cover."

"And you think Laguardia might go underground?"

It was an interesting idea, that he might go some-place we'd never find him. Undercover. He'd never pay for his crimes, but technically, if he stopped committing them, that would at least be an improvement. Still, it wouldn't reflect well on the Bureau for him to slip away—again. Besides, criminals usually needed to keep committing crimes due to whatever compulsion had led them to start.

Brody's voice dropped to a murmur. "This isn't public knowledge yet, but Daniel Fuentes, the guy you interviewed?"

My eyes widened. In my mind, a snapshot flashed of a genial Santa Claus in an orange jumpsuit. The image skipped ahead to the soulless blank stare.

"He's dead," I said, already sure. "How?"

"Apparent suicide."

Apparent. "You doubt the conclusion?"

"He was in his cell, alone. Surveillance shows no one went in or out except for the guard who discovered him. And there were no special calls or letters leading up to the event."

"So it's a suicide."

Brody's expression showed doubt. "The timing is suspicious...your recent visit with Hennessey...the upcoming raid. It's a hell of a coincidence."

And Hennessey didn't believe in coincidence.

Was it possible Laguardia had somehow gotten inside? I didn't see how. Maybe Fuentes had been so scared that Laguardia *would* find out that he'd done the deed preemptively. Or maybe he was just fucked up in the head.

What do you remember?

Three little girls in Tijuana.

Brody's expression hardened. "You understand your role here."

The question hit its target, right where it hurt the most. I was the rookie. I was the little girl who turned in her father. I was the guy wearing the red shirt in the sci fi show, only serving one purpose and destined to die.

"Understood," I said tightly.

He nodded. "Dismissed."

I followed after Hennessey, confused and frustrated. I didn't even know what to think about Fuentes. I wasn't sorry he was dead, but if Carlos could reach inside maximum security, we were pretty well fucked.

And the other part, my role. Yeah, that was coming through loud and clear. The rookie. The throwaway. Because I'd never escape my past. Hennessey was still in the hallway when I caught up to him, which meant he must have been waiting for me. He gave me a sideways glance as we continued together.

He muttered under his breath, mimicking Brody's words. "He's moving now, so you move now. Is that supposed to be some fucking law enforcement wisdom? As if I don't have an arrest list a mile longer than he could ever hope for."

Despite the tension of the moment, I had to crack a smile at the blatant competitiveness. In a way, Hennessey was so high above me, so competent that I idolized him. It helped to see him, at least in this moment, a little petty and a lot human.

He glanced at me, his lips twitching. "What are you laughing at?"

I shook my head, my smile fading. "Is it going to be bad? The bust?"

His sigh gave me the answer. "There's always a chance that shit goes wrong. Sometimes we lose an agent. It happens."

Only then did I remember his other rookie partner…who had died.

In the conference room, he began rifling through the papers. We'd need to reevaluate our blind spots without the snipers in place—and we'd have to do it fast.

He spoke without looking up. "Call everyone on the team. And screen them. If someone has taken so much as a Benadryl, they're out. Everyone comes in clearheaded or not at all. If I have to walk in there by myself, that's what I'll do."

"With me."

"What?" he asked absently.

"I'll be there with you."

When he looked up, his eyes were smoky. Something was there, just behind the mist, but I couldn't read him. "Right," he said finally.

I tried to ignore the unease that pooled in my stomach as I left to make the calls. Thankfully, with the time still early evening, most of the team was available to come in immediately. Unfortunately, I couldn't reach Lance at all. His number went straight to voicemail, as if his phone were off. Frankly, it didn't really matter. He didn't play a pivotal role in the original plan, and considering his rookie status, that likely wouldn't have changed in the rushed new plan.

So what the hell are you doing here? But I didn't have an answer for that.

It took me most of the hour we had left to organize everyone's new assignments. The cubicles and conference room, which had been empty, now bustled with agents. Some prepared to work from the office or in the van to help coordinate. The ones going in suited up in bulletproof gear.

I hadn't donned my gear yet, not wanting the encumbrance before I had to. There was no time to change clothes, so I was stuck in a blue dress shirt beneath my standard suit jacket and skirt. A black T-shirt and black cargo pants were laid out on my bed at home, useless now. I wasn't sure what to do about that, but I was too busy to worry about it. At one point, literally running to get schematics from one end of the office to the other. It hurt on my two-inch heels, even with the fancy insoles I used. Everyone was running around. All our carefully laid plans were out the window, left only with this. Hennessey had been spot on when he'd predicted this would be a clusterfuck. We hadn't even left the building and it already was.

I had glimpsed Hennessey throughout the frenetic planning, but he was always talking to someone. Occasionally he barked out orders to me, and I'd scurry off. More his personal assistant than a partner, but I didn't mind. I believed in what we were doing. I believed in *him*. If anyone could pull this off, he could.

But when he found me, with only thirty minutes before we had to move out, he looked more pissed off than ever. "I need to speak with you."

I glanced down at the armful of portable radios I held, ready to be passed out. "Sure. Can I find you in a few minutes?"

"No. Right now."

Something like dread settled in my stomach. I dumped the equipment on the nearest desk and followed him back to Brody's office. My dread increased.

Sitting inside was Lance. He didn't meet my eyes.

"Is it true?" Brody asked. "Never mind. I already know it's true." He let out a string of profanities a sailor would be proud of.

I stared at Lance in shock. He'd *told?* I knew I'd have to tell Hennessey eventually, but I'd have broken the news carefully—certainly not right before a huge bust. And going to Brody directly was a dick move. At least Hennessey had asked for a replacement to my face. Lance wouldn't even meet my eyes. The moment stretched out.

Betrayed.

I'd been betrayed by my friend. While I had betrayed

my partner. I'd hurt and been hurt. I couldn't think of anything to say to fix this. *I'm sorry.* But I wasn't. It had been the right thing to do. Even if it hadn't resulted in any direct information, it was good to cover our bases. And Mia *had* given me insight into our enemy. So what was the goddamn harm? Except I couldn't ask that question either.

Hennessey broke the ice, but his words chilled me even further. "She stays in the van."

Brody nodded, as if it was decided.

I whirled on my so-called partner. "What the hell? *She?* Why are you talking about me like I'm not here?"

"Fine," he bit out. "You. You stay in the van. For deliberately going against my orders. For sneaking around—"

I made a dismissive sound, cutting him off. I knew it wasn't a good idea to piss him off further, but he'd already taken away what I most wanted: a real spot on his team. A true position as his partner. But that was never going to happen, and it had nothing to do with Mia Martinez. It was about Hennessey not trusting me. If we'd truly been partners, he wouldn't have forbidden me to see her in the first place. What would it take to earn his trust? It didn't matter. I didn't have it now, when it counted most.

"It was the right thing to talk to her, and you know it. I did it on my own time, so as not to interfere with anything you wanted to do. And regardless, talking to her has nothing to do with my ability to execute this bust with you. I know the plan better than any other agent out there."

Hennessey's gray eyes were cool. "Then you'll be an asset directing from the van."

Fuck. *Fuck.* There was no way to win this argument. My first game, and I'd been benched before it started. Worst of all, I'd let Hennessey down. Lance wouldn't look at me, which was probably a good thing since my glare could cut glass. Only Brody looked pleased. He hadn't wanted me out there, I realized.

Strange, considering.

CHAPTER EIGHT

I HAD TO run to catch up with Hennessey. His long legs carried him faster than I could really walk in my low-heeled pumps, but I didn't care how I looked to nosy eyes.

"*Hennessey.* Wait."

His broad back retreated farther down the hall, farther away from me.

"Please, Ian."

He slowed. He had once called after me the same way. Using my first name like a hook, reeling me in. He stopped and turned to face me, giving me that much at least.

"I'm sorry," I said, and as I said the words, they became true. They had always been; I'd just refused to acknowledge how shitty I felt—even to myself. Sure, I'd justified my actions under the umbrella of professional duty, but I owed an even deeper allegiance to the man who had given me his trust. Not even Brody, who most likely had his own agenda. Hennessey was the one who had treated me as though I had value, asking for my opinions and really listening. Ian Hennessey, the man behind the commendations.

I lowered my eyes. Not avoidance. Shame. I lowered my voice too. "I'm really sorry I disobeyed you."

"Disobeyed me?" he snapped. "I'm not the fucking master of you."

He blew out a breath, his frustration obvious. With a tilt of his head, he led me into the supply closet. The same place we'd spoken before. The place we had kissed. Though it was clear kissing wouldn't be on the agenda today based on the rigid way he held himself.

"Look," he continued more evenly, "what happened in there, benching you, it's not about punishment. I just... I can't deal with the implications right now, right before an op. Whether I can trust you or if something bigger is going on. I can't be wondering about that while I'm there or someone will get hurt. We'll work it out after this. I promise."

Jesus. Him being reasonable was like salt on the wound. My voice came out small. "We'll still be partners."

"Yes. Probably."

I sucked in a breath. Well, points for honesty, I guess. But damn, my shame increased by the second. "I'm sorry," I repeated lamely.

He shook his head, his expression softening. "What did she tell you?"

Mia, he meant.

"She said..." I struggled for something useful to share. Even though I appreciated the insight she'd given me, I had to admit it wasn't directly applicable to an impeding attack. "She said they understood each other," I continued cautiously. "That he had a darkness inside him, like hers."

He stared at me blankly. Okay, that had been pretty vague.

"And she said that he would lash out if we got close." And we were about to get very close, right up into his business. "So be careful," I finished softly. "I wish I could be there to have your back, but I understand why I can't."

I felt the tension inside him, some internal battle I wasn't privy to. But he didn't look pissed anymore, so I wasn't going to question it.

"There's a lot of firepower on our side," he said. "And I'll probably work better without worrying what trouble you're getting into."

I gave him a sad smile, aware it didn't really reach my eyes. "Come back to me in one piece, okay?"

It felt chilly, exposing myself that way. Admitting my feelings for him went beyond the professional, even though I'd done so without words. Even if he'd already admitted as much to me with his kiss in this very room. But my feelings went beyond the physical as well, and his eyes darkened with the knowledge.

"Samantha, I..." He stopped himself, looking frustrated and a little bit lost.

It made me want to soothe him. It made me want to keep him safe, as if I could. Except I wouldn't have his back in the raid tonight. Other agents would. More experienced agents would, and that should give me ease—but it didn't. I'd come to care for him more than I'd have thought possible in a few weeks' time. I didn't want him rushing into dangerous situations. Hell, I didn't want him leaving my side at all.

But none of my wishes would come true. He'd go to the warehouse tonight without me. And when this case was over, he'd move on to the next one. Without me.

He cupped my face, his eyes searching mine. I felt infinitely delicate when he held me like this, as if I were made of porcelain and spun gold instead of flesh and blood. As if I might break. His thumb ran along my cheek, softly, gently, the callused pad of his thumb catching my skin, tugging it, abrading it, sandpaper against silk.

He leaned toward me, and this time our kiss was slow, like the long incline of a warm beach with lazy waves, with languid caresses of his mouth on mine. His tongue nudged my lips, and I opened for him. Relaxed against him, submitting myself to the sweet torture of an unhurried kiss.

It was quicksand, swallowing me whole, one small inch at a time. His hand caught my neck from behind, supporting me, holding me steady for his exploration. He tasted of spiced masculinity with a hint of coffee. My tongue darted into his mouth, seeking more—more of his flavor, his heat. More of the heady pleasure coursing through me.

His hands roamed to my side, my back. They burned

through the silk. They scorched my skin. They blazed a path right to my heart—with their odd courtly respect and irrepressible desire. I would never be the same, I realized. Such a small moment to capture such a huge shift.

His hand on my waist.

His lips over mine.

The dust of a thousand files floating all around us like snowflakes.

I loved him then—and looking back, I would always remember the time before that kiss and the time after. Two separate versions of myself, one needy and one fulfilled. He pulled back enough to place warm kisses along my lips with a reverence that undid me.

Over. It was over, but I could still feel him every place that his body touched mine. I still felt breathless and yearning inside. He stepped back with a strange expression. Regretful, almost. And the way his thumb brushed my parted lips before he turned to leave the room...

I stood there, disconcerted and overwhelmed. And suddenly afraid, because that final touch had felt somehow like an apology.

Like saying goodbye.

❖   ❖   ❖

STATIC CRACKLED OVER the radio waves. It felt like the noise inside me, absorbed into my bloodstream, pulse harsh and erratic. He'd said benching me wasn't about punishment, and he wasn't the sort of man to spare my feelings, but it still felt like a punishment.

The A/C on the van rumbled at full blast, but it couldn't penetrate the stale lukewarm air. With Lance and the comm specialist beside me, there was barely room to breathe. I took off my suit jacket, and that helped. But between the thick suit skirt and my pantyhose, my body was boiling itself.

"North team, check."

"Southwest, clear."

Each of the teams reported in from their vantage points, while I waited, holding my breath. The sound came through the speakers. On the panels we could see their locations with red lights overlaid by a map of the docks.

"Are we a go?" Lance asked beneath his breath.

I shook my head. "Not yet. The teams in the water need to report in, and then he goes in."

He was Special Agent Hennessey, the leader of this operation. He'd be leading in the first strike as well, the most dangerous position. Fuck. He'd barely been recognizable on the way over, decked out in his black cargo pants and T-shirt, his shoulder and ankle holsters, his earpiece in and rifle loaded. A bulky bulletproof vest and body armor. With his visor flipped down, he was simply another agent, another man on the ground. A pawn.

If he were hurt tonight, I would blame myself. Even though I likely couldn't protect him, even though the people with him were better trained in combat, stronger fighters, I felt a connection with him. It was damned inconvenient.

"In place," came Hennessey's low assurance over the radio. Without identification, I recognized his voice. We all did.

"Comm here," I said into the mic. "We're all set."

Hennessey's reply came quickly. "Go."

There was a shuffle, and then the comm line dropped. I stared at the blinking equipment, tasting bile in my throat. Just like that, they were walking into a minefield. Radio silence until they were already in and had secured the location. Seconds ticked by. It felt like forever. My muscles were tensed, as if I were in combat, sitting still. My only consolation was the tripwire didn't sound, so they must have cut through the alarm as planned.

A drop of sweat worked its way down the center of my back, a combination of stress and the oppressive atmosphere inside the van. Lance was breathing shallowly, his eyes alert. The comm specialist was busy fiddling with dials I couldn't decipher. The seconds ticked by with excruciating slowness. Five minutes, then six. Life or death in each second.

I'd never really understood when people talked about the condition of human frailty. As if life were spun like glass, but I knew that wasn't right. I knew how much a person could withstand. People had always terrified me, with their ability to hurt other people, with their propensity for not giving a shit. But now I understood how fragile a body was, when I loved the heart beating inside it. The bulletproof vest was little armor against a maniac, one who had no compunction about killing a law enforcement officer.

"Clear."

At that one word, I breathed a deep lungful of humid air. Clear. He was safe. Jesus. Relief flooded my veins, making me lightheaded. Or maybe that was the unfortunate conditions. Either way, I had to close my eyes before speaking again.

Are you okay? I wanted to ask. "Sitrep?" I asked instead. Situation report. *Keep it professional.* At least, while there were twenty other agents on the line.

"About fifteen suspects. Heavily armed. We got here in time."

He meant they'd caught them before the deal went through. Carlos's men in custody, the drugs seized. It was a win. A major win, even if Carlos wasn't among the men there.

"Carlos?" I asked.

"Not sure. We'll have to interview them when we book them."

"Understood. I'll contact base." I was under strict orders to report back to Brody. Then again, I'd proven I wasn't always keen on following orders to the letter. In this case, it seemed fair enough.

"Wait," Hennessey said.

There were low voices over the mic, too soft to make

out. It sounded like he was talking to someone else. I paused, waiting. Then a shout came, as if from some-place away from him. Another shout.

Something was wrong.

"Hennessey," I said, too softly for him to hear me, afraid I'd distract him at some crucial moment.

A loud sound crashed through the speakers just be-fore everything went dark.

"*Ian!*"

Too late. He was gone. The whole system had gone quiet. The comm guy practically shit his pants, cycling through the frequencies, trying to pick it back up. Lance was muttering *fuck fuck fuck* under his breath. I was completely still, processing. Whatever had happened over there, it was bad. Really bad. My imagination filled in the radio silence, envisioning Carlos lined up against the wall with other rough criminals. He would have realized he was caught, that even if he played dumb, we'd be able to figure out his true identity. Cornered, he'd done the only thing he knew how to do—he'd fought his way out. And Hennessey had been talking to me. He'd been distracted.

Lance had it right. *Fuck.*

I was out of the van before I realized what I was doing, pushing through the double-wide doors and breathing in cool, misty air. It had rained. In the forty-five minutes we'd been cooped up inside the bulletproof van, it had rained and I hadn't even realized it. I looked out over the plains and long dirt road, over the tin roofs of the dockside warehouses, and felt a million miles away from Hennessey.

I started for the cluster of buildings when something caught my elbow. No, some*one*.

Lance frowned down at me. Only then did I realize he was taller than me. The way he held himself was usually lower, designed to draw less attention to himself. But that was changing. When he'd stood up to Tyler Martinez on our unauthorized field trip, I'd seen another side of him. That side was gradually coming out more, and I'd be glad for it, once this was all over. Right now, he needed to stand aside.

"Let go of me," I demanded.

"We're supposed to stay in the van."

"Bullshit. They could be in trouble."

"And you're going to help them with what? Your service weapon?"

Good point. They had high-powered assault rifles and body armor. I had a Glock. Still, no way was I sitting still while our men were possibly getting killed.

"I'm going in. Bottom line. These are our people, and they might need us. You're not going to change my mind, so the question is, are you going to help me?"

To his credit, Lance deliberated for only a second. He nodded, and with a quick glance at the van, we slipped along the path and stole behind the nearest building. It was still easily a mile's distance between our location and the main warehouse. This late in the day, the sun was almost horizontal with the ground. It cast a blinding orange glow everywhere it could reach. The other sides of the buildings lay in shadows.

When I reached the main cluster of buildings, I paused at the corner.

Clear.

Lance signaled me ahead while he provided cover, and I returned the favor at the next building. It would go faster if we could run straight through the main streets, but we had no idea what enemies might be waiting in the wings. Even our own people might shoot first and ask questions later if they were in the middle of a firefight.

Sprinting, I rounded a Dumpster and pulled up short beside the building. I breathed hard and waited for Lance to catch up with me.

He didn't.

Peeking around the Dumpster, I called out in a low voice. "Lance? You there?"

Silence. First the team went silent, now Lance. It was starting to become a problem. No, scratch that. It was already a huge fucking problem.

I crept near the dark side of the wall, moving quietly and quickly. I had to hope Lance had made an unfortunate wrong turn. I prayed I'd get a chance to tease him about it. Because if he'd run into someone…if I really lost him…

I rounded the corner where I'd last seen him. Empty. I was alone. I *should* have been alone, but I wasn't. I felt someone watching.

"Lance," I whispered.

The hair on the back of my neck rose. Fear. Real fear. There wasn't time to savor it. I heard the faintest rasp of a rough indrawn breath. Not mine. Gasping, I turned to run. Something heavy slammed into me from behind. I fell, face-first, into the brick wall. My arms wrenched behind my back. I called out, but no one was there. Just my assailant, and he worked quickly and efficiently to subdue me. A prick of pain entered my neck.

A sedative, I realized as the numbness spread over me.

My assailant set me gently on the ground, guiding my fall as my legs stopped working. He turned me over so I was looking up at the orange and purple sunset. His head and shoulders were a silhouette, blocking the light. Even now, I couldn't get a good look at him. Even now, he used the elements against me, keeping me in the dark.

CHAPTER NINE

A T FIRST I assumed it was a dream. My mind felt hazy, my body sluggish. My eyes were closed, with vague lights behind my eyelids, like a tilting, spinning ride at a carnival late at night. I felt like throwing up, and I tried to lurch up, to get out of bed. Except I wasn't on my bed. And my arms didn't move.

And when I opened my eyes, the world was still black.

A blindfold covered my eyes. It trapped my eyelashes back and forth as I blinked helplessly. Thick fabric stretched tight enough to block most of the light. I searched desperately for some glimmer of light peeking from below, where the cloth ran over the bridge of my nose, but the pinkish glow didn't tell me anything. For all I knew it was the inside of my eye or some misfiring of my cornea. I couldn't even trust my senses right now. Even my body had turned against me.

My arms were bound behind my back. The rope scratched at my skin, but didn't chafe too badly as long as I didn't struggle. There wasn't much give though. I pulled carefully at my bonds, which only succeeded to make grooves in my wrist and yank my shoulder.

Captured. Fuck.

Resigned for the moment, I laid down my head. That was the most ridiculous part, the bed. The soft, sweet-smelling bed that I could lounge in for days, for weeks—forever. Sleep seemed like the best possible thing that could happen to me now. Just drift away and never wake up, drowned in a luxury too good for me.

I lay there, unable to move my hands or my legs. Unable to see. Alone with my thoughts.

God, my thoughts. The very thing I'd been running from my entire life. But I would never escape. Especially now at a standstill. Full stop.

To anyone outside, my father must have looked like a good man. He worked all day at a nearby garage as a mechanic, then came home to make dinner for his motherless little girl. He racked up those single father sympathy points. He wasn't bad looking either, judging by the women that would sometimes come around with lasagna and pointed questions about when he'd be home. Little did they know he was out stalking his latest victim. They never suspected just how perverted and deadly his preferences ran. He would be out until late while I huddled in my princess bed.

I loved that princess bed. My dad had taken me to pick it out. In the furniture store there were rows upon rows of king-sized mattresses of varying thickness and softness and material. A hundred different options for adults to pick from, the most expensive of which cost the same as a small car.

For children, there was only one. One brand and one type. Twin-sized. Even rich people were content to let their kids sleep on whatever-the-fuck.

But I'd seen this bed with large looping wheels made of metal and a sheer pink cloth draped over the top, and I'd begged my father. To this day, I don't know why he gave it to me. Or why he'd even care what I wanted. Was he crazy only some of the time? Was his violence reserved for people not related to him by blood? If so, I'd fucked that up by tattling on him. He'd attacked me in the jail just fine.

I slept on the princess bed until the day Child Protective Services took me away. The foster homes weren't as nice, of course. I had old, lumpy mattresses, some of them lousy with fleas. I had foster "brothers" who smirked at me when I got out of the shower and threatened to join me in bed that night. But they never did. It was a shitty environment and a shitty life, but no one ever hurt me.

Until now. Until someone had drugged and kidnapped me. Until he'd tossed me on the softest, most luxurious bed I'd ever imagined. The irony was almost enough to kill me, and I prayed it would, really. I'd looked at enough case photos to know what lay in store for me. I remembered the blood on my father's hands. This wouldn't end prettily or without pain, and I was helpless to change my fate. Maybe I always had been.

A sound caught my attention, the gentle squeak of hinges followed by booted feet on hardwood. My mind sketched in the picture, starting with me and radiating outward. Blindfolded and bound. Fully dressed, as far as I could feel. No, wait. My jacket was gone. No bulk around my shoulders. The tautness around my chest felt like my bra and dress shirt. The skirt was there too, thick and unwieldy as ever. Between my ankles, I felt the thin netting of my pantyhose.

I heard him coming. A man approaching, a quiet one. He stalked me. Maybe my mind was adding that element, because I felt so much like prey. But his step was fast enough to be purposeful and slow enough to be predatory.

My heart beat so wildly, and irrationally, I felt sure he must hear it. I swallowed thickly against the dryness in my throat, and I was certain he heard that too. Every brush of my sleeve against the bedspread, every throb of discomfort in my shoulder. Every sound and sensation magnified under the weight of sensory deprivation and pure, absolute fear.

A gentle hand brushed back the hair from my face. It tickled, and on instinct, my nose scrunched. He laughed softly. Oh God. I was amusing him. He thought I was cute. This was some sort of twisted flirtation, a touch and a response. An advance and a surrender.

"Special Agent Samantha Holmes," I said between clenched teeth, rattling off my badge number. Name, rank, and serial number. In case this guy was sane enough to care about the punishment for cop killing.

Fuck you, I added silently.

He didn't laugh this time. At the first touch of his hand, I flinched away. But I only succeeded in pressing myself against the impossible plushness beneath me. He stroked my hair again, fingering the strands softly before letting them drop. He was exactly as gentle as the first time. Almost caring.

Don't engage. That was standard operating procedure for a prisoner of war—and the drug trade was war. *Wait for rescue.* Yeah, that was un-fucking-likely. I could be almost anywhere by now. In a room with a bed wasn't exactly specific. Besides, I sensed he was something else, and I was too, like maybe this was personal. And that had a totally different set of rules. *Reach out, humanize yourself, make him want to help you.*

But either way, one thing was clear. If I had the chance to escape, I would take it. That chance didn't have to be large. It could be a single hand free, jamming his throat into the footboard of the bed until he passed out. It could mean running away from a man with a gun and letting him shoot me in the back. Criminals had been resorting to *suicide by cop* for decades. Only fair I could turn the tables if I needed to. I had no idea what this man would do to me, but it seemed likely that by the end I'd rather be dead.

An evil sociopath. A young woman. Fill in the blanks. Unimaginable horrors visited upon my body were practically mandatory.

So why did I feel a budding sense of relief? I struggled to contain it. Could he see it on my face? What sort of twisted, fucked up…but I already knew the answer to that. I'd been like this from the moment I'd turned in my dad. No, earlier. When I'd seen the blood on his hands, and I'd known. *I am in a family of crazy people.*

I am crazy.

The textbooks couldn't say that. The criminal behaviorists and the psychologists didn't know either. *Survivor's guilt.* Fucking clueless. They wouldn't know crazy if it tied them up and stroked their faces, but I did. Oh, I felt it too. Shimmery and translucent, like looking in a mirror. Like being made of glass.

"Let me go," I said, surprised at how bold I sounded. Unafraid. And why shouldn't I be? What could he do to me, except what I'd always wanted? "You won't get away with this. The FBI will find you."

"Shhh." He touched his finger to my lips in a sensual parody of a comforting motion. Not resting his finger across my lips, the way people usually did. He ran his forefinger across the seam of my lips, sending small tingles through my sensitive skin. What a crazy fucker.

But he didn't know who he was dealing with. I could give as well as take. I bit him. I *bit* him, feeling his flesh give between my teeth, tasting the faint salt and musk of a clean man. A soft exhalation escaped him, part pain and part surprise. The callused pad of his finger rasped across my tongue. Like a dog with a bone, I wasn't letting go.

He pinched the bridge of my nose. I bit down harder, sucking air into my mouth around the sides of his finger. It wasn't enough, though. Dizzy, I opened my mouth to breathe in deeper, and he was free. In seconds, my small rebellion had been crushed. Rendered ridiculous. Only, why hadn't he slapped me? Punched me? I would have let go of his finger in the face of violence, whether from shock or submission. But he hadn't hurt me. Just done the bare minimum so I'd let him go.

He didn't punch me now either, in punishment. He could have, and I probably deserved it, by the rules of this messed up captivity game. I hadn't broken skin, but I wouldn't be surprised if he had a black and blue ring around his forefinger tomorrow.

"So fierce," he whispered, stroking my hair again.

And God. God. Why was he so gentle with me? His touch, the bed? It was a perversion, this kindness. A hardworking single father who killed in his spare time. A kidnapper who petted me and gave me luxuries I'd never afforded myself. The world had turned upside down, the sky underneath me while I looked up at the glistening sea.

"Please." Less brave now. Was that my voice? More like a whimper. "Just let me go. Tell me what you want from me. Leave me alone."

Three different requests. I was panicking. I recognized it with a kind of detached calm. One part of my mind was thoughtful, examining my predicament with professional precision. The other part was flipping the fuck out, an animal with her back against the wall. I jerked in my bonds, accomplishing nothing. I wriggled again, knowing I looked ridiculous and not giving a shit.

Fear had a taste, I discovered. Harsh and metallic. Like blood. I'd first tasted it in the surveillance van when I'd thought Hennessey was in trouble. *He still might be in trouble.*

"Fuck," I panted. "Let me go."

"You'll be fine," he murmured, his voice barely above a breath. The only clue to his identity was the slightest hint of an accent. "I promise."

My laugh cut the air, bitter. "Oh, you promise. I don't even know you. I can't trust you."

"You can. I may not answer every question. You may not like what I say. But here, in this room, it will always be the truth."

His voice rang with sincerity. *Impossible.* And yet, the offer was too seductive to ignore. I could ask him anything and hear the answer. What would we ask if we could be sure to know the truth? I found myself quiet. The truth had always been terrifying. I'd learned early on not to ask questions.

This will be our little secret, okay?

As a child, my ignorance had been an uncomfortable sort of bliss. And the truth had set me free, but only in the most painful ways. I'd been alone in the world, tossed with one indifferent family after another. The truth wasn't what I really wanted from him, but it was all he was offering.

"Is he alive?" My voice came low and thready. I was afraid to know the answer.

"Who? Your partner?"

I flinched beneath the blindfold. "The man who was with me at the docks."

"Ah, that one. Very much alive, last I heard. He was wearing a vest. Unlike you."

Relief. Because Lance *had* worn his vest. Had he been shot because he wouldn't die? No, I was giving my captor too much credit. He didn't care about Lance's life. He wouldn't care about mine.

"Are you going to let me go?"

"Eventually."

Most kidnapping victims died within the first twenty-four hours. "Are you going to rape me?"

"No. Not until you ask me to."

Then it wouldn't be rape, his tone implied. But we both knew otherwise. I was his captive, under his control. There were thousands of ways a person could be made to do something they didn't want to. Ways a person could be made to *ask* for something they didn't want. Coercion. Blackmail. Persuasion. Which ways would he choose?

Deep breath. "Are you going to hurt me?"

"Only as much as I need to."

Which meant yes. As horrible as it sounded to be hurt, there was a relief as well. At least this time I wouldn't be spared. There was also a glimmer of hope with how regretful he sounded. Maybe he didn't want to hurt me. Maybe it was something we could talk about. *Negative transference.* That was another fancy buzzword the textbook left me with. He didn't want to hurt me. He wanted to hurt *himself.* Yeah, I was sure that would go over great with a sociopath.

Last question.

"Are you Carlos?"

Silence. I thought for a moment he'd invoke that privilege he'd been careful to retain, not to answer certain questions. Or maybe put me on the defensive with his many aliases, Carlos Laguardia, or Matthew Genner, or William Hernandez. That he'd staunch the trickle of information altogether, but in the end, he did none of that. He told the truth.

"Yes," he finally said. "But then you knew that. You knew the answer to all these questions. You just wanted reassurance. Put your mind at ease, little one. You'll be tortured here. That's what you wanted to know, isn't it?"

Tears leaked from my eyes, dampening the cloth across them. He was right, and I hated that he was right. I hated that I'd always escaped every horrible scenario and that I'd never had the strength to hurt myself instead. I looked at cutters with longing, those who could inflict brutal self-harm. Even people with anorexia caused long-term damage to their bodies.

I'd never been able to do those things. I just chased after bad guys, like Carlos, and hoped they'd be as horrible as their reputations demanded. That was the only way I'd ever atone for not turning my father in sooner. It was the only way I'd atone for turning him in at all.

Survivor's guilt. That wasn't the half of it.

"I'm going to break you," he continued. "Until you look to me for food, for pleasure, for survival. And the truth is, I'm never letting you go. Not really. You'll walk around outside this place, away from me, but no matter where you go, I'll always be here." He tapped my temple gently. "I'll always be with you."

Was that supposed to be terrifying or comforting? I wasn't sure which way I felt either. Both, maybe.

"I'll punish you for every lie you ever told, for everything you ever took that you didn't really deserve. For every single thing you've ever felt guilty for. But there's a price. You can't be a regular person when we do that. We can't hold onto decorum and manners and cut you open, raw and bleeding, can we?"

And I realized then that Mr. Hyde wasn't really evil personified. He was a man without decorum or manners. He was raw and bleeding, all over. He was me, inside this cell. I couldn't control this shift any more than Dr. Jekyll could. I could only react, only feel pain and anger and fear. And in the end, if the darkness ever lifted?

Dr. Jekyll hadn't been able to live with himself.

Laguardia continued stroking my hair, softly, innocently. My eyelids grew heavy beneath the blindfold, my limbs relaxed in their binds. Exhaustion crept over me like night blanketing the earth, dark and peaceful. *Sleep*, his touch told me, *and I will watch over you until morning.* The same promise made by the moon. But neither Laguardia nor the moon would keep me safe. No one could promise that, least of all a madman, a man pulled by the tides of cruelty. I succumbed anyway, drifting in an inky ocean and lulled to sleep by a killer.

My killer.

CHAPTER TEN

I WOKE UP choking, drowning. With a painful gulp, I swallowed my own spit, struggling to close my mouth around the obstruction and failing. A gag. Round, rubbery. I flicked it with my tongue, but it didn't budge. My jaw already ached and I wondered how long it had been there, how long I had been out. Time passed like lights blinking through a tunnel, a flash and then another until they blended into each other. Fitting, because I was underground now, traveling at high speeds, forced to follow this path to its end.

Where are we? I wanted to ask, but instead I just managed to mumble, "Mmmmf."

A blindfold still covered my eyes, but it had shifted enough where I could see through the bottom. Yellow light concentrated to my right side. A lamp. On a bedside table, maybe. The room as a whole was dark, but when he turned toward me, I caught the impression of brown eyes, almost black. Of a shadow of growth on his jaw. Of a terrifying half smile on his lips. I shut my eyes quickly, not wanting him to catch a glimpse of my eyes open.

Too late. He tugged on the blindfold and my sight

was gone. My cheeks heated from being caught. I squirmed in place. Air kissed my skin, awakening every sense. I was naked, while the part I most wanted uncovered, my eyes, were blind.

Powerless. He wanted me to feel powerless.

The part of me that had trained to deal with criminals like him tried to reason it out. To make a mockery of him the way he'd made a mockery of me. He clearly had a small ego if he needed to exert control over someone less strong than him. Maybe his mother had ignored him. Or he had a tiny penis and the boys at school had mocked. There was always a reason. It didn't excuse his behavior, but it explained it. Like a puzzle piece fitting into place. I just had to find the crazy-shaped square and I'd stop feeling so fucking terrified. I'd stop trembling.

No one had ever hurt me, but that was about to change.

A brush against my ankle was almost too light to feel. But I did feel it, and I knew that my pantyhose were gone. When had he taken them off? I tensed, straining, focusing on the tender flesh. Light fingers ran up the arch of my foot to the inside of my ankle. Over and back, across the bone that jutted there.

"So pretty. So delicate. So easy to break."

I jerked against the bonds, the ones that held my legs down and my arms up. Oh God. To break me as a person? To break my *ankle*? Either one was pretty horrifying. What a sick fuck. A really sick fuck with a tiny penis and an emo sob story. He was just like every other criminal on the fucking Most Wanted wall at the Bureau. He was *nothing*.

But that was a lie I told myself. Because I'd always known he was different. Smarter. More deliberate. He toyed with the FBI like a lion with a mouse, and even as the mouse stared into the jaws of its killer, it felt a little impressed. A little in awe.

The hand smoothed up my calf. His thumb and forefinger framed my kneecap and stroked it. Not causing me pain, but firmly enough to replay the words in my head. *So easy to break.* If he tried to torture information out of me, how long until I gave in?

Not long, I feared. Once a man gave up decorum and manners, it wasn't a huge step to giving up honor too. His. Mine. It blended together in a flow of molten fear, incinerating everything in its path.

"Be a good girl for me, and no one gets hurt. Not you. Not, what was his name? Lance." The pause felt heavy, poignant. His voice dropped. "Not your partner either."

A shiver ran through me. *What did he know about my partner?* Knowledge could be dangerous. It could be used against me.

Did he know I cared about Hennessey?

"He's very worried about you," he said, taunting me.

At least that meant he was alive. Behind the blindfold, I could see his slight smile. Beneath the soft scent of roses, I could smell the clean-sweat smell of him. The ghost of him stood close so close I could feel him, right in front of me, and a small sound came from my throat—fear, frustration. Longing.

"Are you worried about him?" The air brushed my cheek as he leaned close. "You should be. He's playing a dangerous game. One wrong move, and he'll end up dead. But you don't want that to happen, do you? Do you think you can save him?"

His broad hand cupped the inside of my thigh. Sparks radiated from his hand, sending small shocks through my leg, tensing my stomach. And *there*, I felt a strange and undignified heat begin to form. Physical awareness. Proximity. The body's natural defense to an encroaching threat. A woman's natural response to ten thousand fucking years of male dominance. I made excuses for myself, but in the end, I still felt guilty for the clenching of my cunt.

The term *survivor's guilt* had never felt more appropriate than now. This was how I would survive. By preparing myself for him. By wanting it. And why shouldn't I feel guilty for that? It was sick, and so was I. But as long as I was good for him, no one would get hurt.

Hennessey wouldn't get hurt.

"The skin here is paler than anywhere else on the body. Do you agree?"

The muscles of my thigh bunched. God. I wished he'd do something extreme. Just beat me or whip me. Just get it over with. The waiting was torture. The gentle touching.

"So easy to mark," he said, but before I could register the words, a blinding pain racked my body. I gasped, unable to breathe or think. Even when I felt the pressure ease, pain sang a red-haze song through my blood.

He touched the hot points of flesh where his fingers had dug in. "One, two, three. They're red now, but I think they'll turn black and blue before this is over. You'd like that, wouldn't you? To prove how hard you worked for it. You'd press them when I wasn't here and get wet for me."

You're sick, I wanted to say. "Mmmf!" A line of drool leaked from the corner of my mouth and ran down my cheek.

His fingers roamed upward, probing the lips of my cunt. Without preamble, they slid inside. I gasped, sucking in my own spit and swallowing to clear it. His fingers were blunt and unkind and knowledgeable. They knew the angle of a woman and the place deep inside to seek out. He finger-fucked me until I bit down around the gag and stiffened my body against the oncoming tension. Physical awareness. Proximity. The body's natural defense. That was all it was.

He pulled out just as suddenly as he'd started, and my flesh closed around the space left behind. His fingers walked up my quivering belly, leaving wet dots from his fingertips, my own body's response in humiliating points. Past my belly button. My anxiety rose with each small step, as his fingers dried on my skin. He walked his fingers until they reached the curve between my breasts.

I breathed so hard and so fast that I panted. I struggled to suck in air through my nose and around the gag. The world went hazy and dim. I was going to faint...but I didn't. That would be too damn easy. Instead, I just lay there, having a nervous breakdown while he touched me in a single place. My breastbone, like pointing at someone, like accusing them.

Stop, I wanted to say. "Mmmf..." A muffled plea, like a sheep bleating on its way to the slaughter.

"Yes, you're right. Enough of that. We have things to do. Very busy."

He stepped away, and I heard rustling. Dread sank in my gut. Whatever was coming next, it would be much worse.

In that hollow minute of uncertainty, an image of Hennessey flashed through my mind. What would he do in this situation? I couldn't imagine him tied up or beaten, but he could have been, just as easily. If the timing were a little different. If Laguardia still wanted to torture a man instead of a woman. I had no doubt that he had tortured his share of men, turned them into Mr. Hydes against their will. Like the good, misguided doctor in the story, we'd drunk the potion, trying to protect mankind from the monsters within us. And created a new monster instead.

A sharp pain sank into my breast, and a sound of surprise escaped me. Surprise and anguish. And relief. God. Finally. It hurt worse than I was expecting, but then it was supposed to. That was what made it punishment. The second strike drew a gasp from me. The third, a soft whine.

I tried to distract myself by imagining what it was. A whip of some kind? No, it wasn't long enough. A flogger, maybe. I could just picture one, with a blunt leather tip.

He worked his way over my breasts. Like a lover would, I realized. Kissing over the tops and working his way inside. Along the tender underside, making me squirm. Saving the tip for last. But there, he paused to caress the hardening nub with cruel heat-filled lashes. The stunted sounds of my pain filled my ears, a high note above the rapid beat of my pounding blood.

He moved down my belly, not pausing there, just slapping my tender flesh to mark the passage. I jerked against my bonds. *There?* No. God no. It would hurt so fucking bad…

But that was what made it a punishment.

There were lies people told you to get you to cooperate. *This won't hurt. It will be over soon.* He didn't bother with those. No. As far as I could tell, he'd told the truth every step of the way. Then again, there were plenty of things he hadn't told me, and a lie of omission was still a lie.

He moved to my feet, and when he hit me again, he used some kind of implement. Something thin and reedy. It felt like the sole of my foot cracked in half, split with a wicked knife. But then he pulled back and the pain faded. And I knew it would come again.

It did. He used that goddamn horrible stick on my feet while my body jerked. It was the most painful thing I'd ever felt—*on my feet*. When my legs were moving spastically, out of my control, he held them down with one hand and hit them some more, picking up the pace. They would be broken, I thought dimly. They would be cut into ribbons.

But then he stopped and in the seconds that passed, the pain in my feet faded to a dull ache. It was a sharp and fleeting hurt, one that took my breath away and left before I reclaimed it.

The next slap was with his hand again, on my thigh, and I had to sigh in relief. *One, two, three.* Even without his words describing it, I knew he found the same places. I wasn't the one obsessed with my bruises—he was. He moved to the other side. My body jerked away, and somehow toward him. It was confused, mistaking the pain for pleasure and the pleasure for affection.

The blindfold and my muteness served as a barrier between us. They were obvious signs of bondage and my captivity. But in another way they allowed me to pretend I was somewhere else. At home, maybe, and I'd finally found a date who could give me everything I wanted. One who'd spiked my drink and pushed me inside my own door. One who'd held down my hands and taken what he wanted. That date had never happened, because no one had ever hurt me.

But he did.

The skin closer to my cunt was more sensitive, and I

couldn't help but cry out. I moved constantly, a puppet on leathery strings. My toes curled in alternating pain and anticipation, and every time they did, I felt an echo of pain from my feet. A warm, lulling fog descended over my mind, hiding before and after, so there was only now, this moment, and all the ways he could make me hurt.

Here, too, he struck me the same way a lover might kiss me. Along the insides of my thighs to start. Then inward, closer. Finally, he moved up and down the lips of my cunt. He reached down to spread those lips and delved deeper with each stinging blow. When he snapped the wet leather against my clit, I screamed.

He hit me there again and again, until all the breath left my lungs, all the thought left my head. I was nothing but sensation, nothing but lights under the tunnel, flashing bright on each new burst of pain. My mouth was open, my body strung taut. I wanted to beg him to stop. But even when he unclasped the gag and pulled it way, my mouth remained open and mute. Accepting this. Needing it. He laid the damp strap across the most sensitive part of me, the only organ built solely for pleasure, and he made it pain.

I choked on my sorrow, my guilt. My moan mingled with his grunts, his low animal sounds on every strike. The strange thing was I sounded like a person being pleasured. The stranger thing was he sounded like someone in pain.

I wondered when he'd stop hitting me, hurting me, but maybe he never would. We'd be caught in a web of our own making, turned monster by a poison we'd created. There was no escaping the trap we had set for ourselves, no believing our own lies. This place was stripped of decorum and manners. All that was left was rawness and blood. My blood. It squeezed through tiny strips made in my skin on my breasts and thighs. I could feel it where the salt of my sweat burned.

Was he waiting for me to come? It would never happen. A sensual tension held me in its grip, but I would never let go enough to enjoy it. There was only pain for me, and that was all I wanted. To enjoy it would have been much worse, and I didn't have to. My body had been played like an instrument. Like an object. And objects didn't come.

Only then did I realize the mockery he'd made of sex. Using the flogger to mimic a lover's exploration. Blocking my senses. Using an object on an object, like making a doll fuck another doll. Was that how he saw himself too, as a thing? Or was he a god, the one orchestrating us all? I knew the truth. Somehow I knew, the same way I'd known he hated the cold. And I knew because even something as cruel as this formed a bond of intimacy between us. The real reason he orchestrated this crimson dance was because it was all he could handle.

He was Mr. Hyde, and if he stopped being evil for just a moment, if the haze of violence cleared, he would see what he'd done. He'd turn into Dr. Jekyll again and then he'd hate himself. He'd kill himself, and in that twisted logic, he hurt me in order to save himself.

"Please," I murmured, exhausted and spent.

"Shhh." He picked me up, and I wavered on my feet.

With his help I stumbled over to a bathroom. He set me down on a toilet and held my face against his leg while I peed. The sound was loud, and I didn't even care. He'd seen me *bleed*, so what did it matter if he saw me pee? He'd torn into my soul; nothing he could do to my body would hurt anymore. That was probably another lie.

He wiped me himself, and I sat blankly as the water ran and he washed his hands. Then he ran a stinging wipe over my cuts. The chemical smell pierced my sinuses. Antiseptic. He was taking care of me, looking after my health. How ironic. I could have laughed. I didn't.

After, he laid me back down on the bed. Under the sheets this time. Not tied up this time.

He climbed in behind me, and for a moment, I was surprised. The haze lifted, and I wondered why a warm, hard body had nestled in around me, the fabric of his shirt soothing on my overheated skin. He was *spooning* me, for Christ's sake. But then I remembered the parody we were making. First came sex and then the cleanup routine. Now would be cuddling.

And pillow talk?

The time when men were vulnerable because they'd just had an orgasm. Except he hadn't come.

"Why are you cold?" I whispered, cringing because I expected a blow. For talking at all or for asking a personal question.

He answered easily, though, as if we *were* lovers instead of a criminal and his pet FBI agent. "A brain injury when I was a child. I'm fine now, but the part of my brain that figures out if you're cold, that makes you put on a jacket or go back inside the house, that part's just broken."

"So your temperature—"

"Is normal. But my brain doesn't know that, so I'll keep wearing layers and turning up the furnace until I overheat myself."

How was that for lies we told ourselves? He couldn't trust the messages his own brain was telling him. And he really had told me the truth. He hadn't even seemed surprised by my question.

It was worth it. The thought came to me suddenly that if I had to endure an hour of pain for a single confession, it was worth it. Not only for the job, but also for myself. Some personal quest I couldn't quite admit yet. And maybe it was a fair trade after all. Who knew what the admission had cost him? He'd sounded so at peace with it, as if remarking on the brown of his eyes or the tan of his skin. And yet, he wouldn't know how to show any weakness. Not this man. He would have been dead by now. By his own hand or someone else's.

I could understand him. I didn't have to like him.

He lay holding me as I drifted off, only the mockery seemed less and less fake. And more real than any embrace I had known. Only then did I remember I'd had my blindfold on. The entire time he flogged me, even in the bathroom. But he'd directed me the entire way. And somehow, I'd pictured him. His body. His face. As if I could see it without looking, so I hadn't even noticed the barrier across my eyes.

Maybe it was his presence—an overriding charisma that would give him the power to speak in a room full of terrifying criminals. The power to rule them. The presence painted a more defined picture than most people's actual appearance did.

Was I in awe of him? Did I like him?

No. He'd been bullied as a kid. He had a small penis. He was overcompensating for something. But the old explanations felt empty now, more of a mockery than his sex-like beating had been. This wasn't a man who reacted to things. He molded the world in his image. He *was* god-like after all, whether he saw himself that way or not. So what did it mean that I was no longer afraid when he held me? The pain warmed me across the front of my body, and he from behind.

Was he cold, though? He might feel that way. I snuggled deeper and tucked the blanket over my shoulder, making sure it covered him too. Jesus, I was comforting my captor. Crazy. Insanity. A madman holding me in bed, and I had to appease him or he'd hurt me again. A lie, but then what was wrong with that? Sometimes you could take comfort in a lie. You could nurture it and hold it close to your heart. Right up until it turned on you.

CHAPTER ELEVEN

M Y BODY DRAPED a bench, hands tied down. Ankles tied down. Cushions supported me. It was almost like a massage chair. Except I wouldn't be getting anything as nice as that. I was naked, blindfolded, gagged. My uniform for my position as his slave. A prerequisite before he would touch me.

And he *was* touching me. Stroking my hair and running his hands down my back. Lightly, like calming a wild animal. Which was crazy, since *he* was the animal. So why was I panting, nostrils flared? Why did an uncontrollable keening sound escape me, a cross between pleasure and despair? With just a gentle touch he could reduce me to my basest state. He could turn me from Jekyll to Hyde. He was my poison.

I sighed, relaxing against the warm padded bench. Relaxing into him, because he pressed me more firmly now, seeking out the knots in my shoulders and rubbing them away. God, he was good at that. We could have been any ordinary couple, the man giving a back rub to the woman. The gentle clink of metal where the cuffs rubbed against their base reminded me that we were different. The pleasure would soon turn to pain.

"Did you miss me?" he asked, speaking low. His words always hovered just above a breath, sharpened by that faint accent. I couldn't even imagine how it would feel for him to speak normally, how much it would cut me open.

Anyone could miss company when they were left alone in the dark.

He chuckled softly. "You're so tense when you're angry."

I stiffened further at his words. But he wouldn't let even that small rebellion go. He pushed the fierceness out of my body with firm strokes. God. All the questions I had bunched up in my hands. *Why are you doing this? Will you ever let me go?* But he'd never tell me the answers to them, and he'd saved us both the trouble by making it so I couldn't ask. I opened my palm, and the questions drifted away, over the wind and out to sea.

You only have this moment, the restraint told me. *You only have what you feel.*

It changed the synapses of my brain. Instead of escape, I wanted to take whatever comfort I could find. Instead of cold professionalism, I wanted to understand where he was coming from. I already *did* understand, deep inside. We were both trapped here. His handcuffs weren't visible, but they kept him bound to me as much as I was trapped against this bench. A man this powerful, this wealthy, this *skilled* at bringing pleasure to a woman didn't need to force one. I was a hassle he didn't need. However unlikely, I might one day escape. Might one day testify against him. Much easier just to pay a woman, to seduce her. And this wasn't a man who took unnecessary risks. But here we were.

Reluctance. Coercion. They strummed through my body—and his.

"Don't worry. I'll start slow." He sounded almost concerned. I could have believed he cared, but for the sting that hit my ass. I gasped against the shock and braced myself for another. His palm landed on my other ass cheek, waking every nerve ending in my body. I recognized the sensation from last time, a tingling warmth. I'd thought I was awake, walking around and going through the motions. But then he spanked me, he whipped me, and I realized that had all been a dream. This was real.

He switched to a flogger, covering my ass cheeks and then working his way up my back. This was new territory, a parallel of what he'd done to the front side of my body. I gritted my teeth and tried not to cry out.

A pause.

This new implement whistled in the air before it landed across my shoulders. *Oh God.* The strands were long and thick. They covered me from spine to shoulder before flicking off again. The pain felt almost less than before. Certainly there was less of a sting. But more of an impact. I felt the thud ripple across my skin and reverberate in my bones. My fear faded under his onslaught, turning into something murkier. Something gray and reflective. Something good.

I understood now what his massage had been. To show me what would come. It felt like a hundred hands pressing into my skin, a thousand minute corrections across my back until my muscles melted into puddles. I was hugging the bench, grateful it could hold me up. Even my brain had turned to mush, entering a strange twilight hour when the sky turned hazy and stars glittered.

My spit pooled behind the ball gag. When I didn't swallow fast enough, a drop leaked from the corner of my mouth. I didn't care. I couldn't, not when I'd found some higher plane, a place where I could float. This wasn't a base place, an animal incarnation. This was strangely spiritual. A perversion, no doubt. Maybe even blasphemy. But so sweet I would want to come here again anyway. I'd sell my soul for this feeling, but then, maybe I already had.

He stopped striking me, but the sensations continued, racing each other over my skin. This felt amazing, and I wanted to ask him why he'd force a woman to take this. He seemed handsome enough, especially if you ignored the crazy dead look in his eyes I'd glimpsed in secret. He had plenty of money. Why not find a woman and make her feel like this? Unless forcing a woman was half the fun.

My job is to put them in handcuffs, not care how they got there.

That was what Hennessey had told me, but he wasn't here now. Not caring how they get there had been a luxury reserved solely for the free. He could put in his hours, make his arrests, and go home at the end of the day.

Not me.

Soft rustling sounds came from behind me. I felt his soft breath on my lower back, and I knew he was crouching down behind me. Something hard and cool prodded my entrance—and pushed inside. He hadn't used lube. It was my body's own preparation, creaming myself in anticipation of him. A defense mechanism, I told myself, but the excuse felt thin. Whatever object he'd put inside me, it stretched me to full capacity.

Cocks would have felt hard in my hands and in my cunt. But they weren't really, were they? They were flesh and blood and muscle. The thing he'd put inside me— that was hard. Made of something with no give at all. Maybe glass. I felt stretched and daunted. *Take it*. With a single thrust, he shoved the dildo all the way inside, and I gasped, feeling its curved tip bottom out at my cervix. My mouth was open around the ball gag, panting against the intrusion. Too full. Too much.

But this wasn't about what I wanted, was it? This was punishment. Except when his fingers found my clit from beneath me, when they circled and teased and drew a stuttering orgasm from me, it didn't feel like a punishment at all. The walls of my cunt clenched around the glass dildo and rained down hot liquid.

The dildo pressed against the forward wall, finding my clit from the other side, making me come even harder. I felt something wet gush out of me, and I worried briefly, *his hand, getting him wet,* before I realized how crazy it was to be worried what he thought. He'd made me do this. It was all for him anyway. So I let myself go, riding the waves of my orgasm, one after the other until I could only rock on the choppy seas, eyes closed against a blinding sunset.

He unlatched the gag and removed it. Gently, he wiped the drool from my face.

"Why are you doing this?" My words came slurred. I sounded drunk, and felt that way too, but this was important. I only had this time, right after he'd hurt me, to ask him questions. It was the eye of the storm.

"Because I can," he said simply. "I don't need another reason."

It wasn't the answer I was looking for, and he knew that. I didn't feel he was evading me either. That was the logic he used to justify it, but deeper still, in the places where logic didn't reign, where instinct did, he *wanted* this. My subjugation. My fear. Elemental, the way another man wanted to kiss or feel a woman up. Just instinct.

"Will you ever let me go?" I asked. He'd already told me. I knew the answer. But I had to find out. Had to hear it again.

"Eventually." His voice was faintly regretful. "If it makes you feel any better, it was decided before I took you. You never stood a chance."

"Why would that make me feel better?"

He ran his thumb over my lips. "Because someone finally wanted you. Not just because you were pretty and convenient. Someone was willing to hurt you. To take that risk. My little orphan with no one to abuse her. To understand her. But I do. You're just as crazy as me, love. And we're going to be happy together for a long fucking time."

I shivered. How could he know that about me? Why would he care? I'd kept my horrible desires hidden from everyone. Even myself. Never admitting, even to myself, that I wanted someone to hit me, stalk me, rape me. I'd never secretly wished the sweet guy I was dating would turn into a raving psycho behind closed doors and make me do things I didn't want. That was crazy.

You're just as crazy as me, love. A sob escaped me, just one. Because he was right. Normal people didn't think like that. Most people avoided becoming a victim. This was why I'd become an agent: to protect them. And to put myself in harm's way. Firemen weren't called crazy for running into fires. Maybe they secretly wanted to burn.

✧ ✧ ✧

SOMETHING WAS DIFFERENT.

For the past three days he had come at every mealtime. He would help me wobble to the bathroom. He would feed me some time-specific meal, so I could get my bearings. Scrambled eggs and toast for breakfast. A hearty stew for lunch. Gnocchi and marinara sauce for dinner with a warm garlic bread that tasted homemade. There was always music for our meals and our sessions. He varied the selection, but he was a fan of *La Bohème*, that much was clear. Really, if it weren't for the chains and the whips, he'd have been a very good host.

But he hadn't come for a while now. Without the meals to tick away the hours, I couldn't tell how long it had been. But I was hungry. And I had to pee.

And pain screamed through my arms at being held in one place for so long.

Fear was a constant presence in my mouth, harsh and metallic. I was worried about nerve damage at this point, and that was unlike him. So far he'd been careful with me. Cuts and bruises, but no broken bones. Nothing permanent.

Permanent. A very scary word to a woman in my position. Permanent damage would mean he never planned to send me back. It was a death sentence.

I squirmed again, wishing I didn't have to pee so badly at such a dire moment. It was very distracting. They don't explain that part in all the dramatic climaxes in plays. When the *Phantom of the Opera* kidnaps Christine and ties her up, they don't show how she used the facilities or when. An oversight, surely, because now that I was here, these struck me as vital plot points.

I must have dozed off, but finally, a sound pierced my hungry, painful fog. A creak. Like the door, but even that sounded different. The steps inside, different.

What if it was someone else?

There was silence, but I felt him watching me. I felt more acute fear in that moment than I had the entire time. Realizing I could get left behind. Having no idea who was looking at me.

Hesitant fingers pulled at the knotting behind my back. My fingers were released, and a thousand needles shot through them. He undid all the rope, at my ankles and beneath my breasts. The numbness turned to a raging fire of pain, and I whimpered. His hands went to my arms, no longer unsure. He massaged my muscles…

And I realized I was free.

No restraints held me down. Even *he* wasn't holding me down, just touching me. Caressing me. Had I heard the door actually close? I wasn't sure.

I lay still, but not too still. It was important not to project. Keep breathing. Don't move.

"Please," I murmured.

He stopped.

I didn't have to pretend my throat was dry. My lips were chapped. "Water," I whispered.

The bed moved as he stood up. It had to be a trap, but I heard his footsteps move away. It had to be a trick, but the faucet squeaked and water rushed. It was too good to be true, but I believed in it anyway. I rushed up, ignoring the fiery pain in my limbs, tilting sideways as the blood rushed to my head. There was no way it should have worked, but it did.

The room came to me in flashes of light. An open-air unfinished space with metal rafters. A raw wooden floor.

Neatly organized implements in the corner. A triangle of light spilling out from the bathroom. Only seconds to get there.

Then I was standing in front of the bathroom, yanking the door shut. For a split second, we were face to face. I stared into startled brown eyes. What I saw there was soulless and cruel, like looking in the mirror. I imagined hurting him. Killing him. I imagined he was my father, and I finally paid him back for what he did to me.

But I'd never had a taste for violence, not really.

I slammed the door shut and shoved the bench underneath it. This bench I had been draped over when he spanked me and fucked me with a dildo. That was the lock to bind him.

The door shuddered as he rammed into it from the other side. He didn't bother yelling for me to undo it. He was smart enough to know better than that.

Something about the situation was off. It was too easy.

Too simple.

Not what I wanted at all.

But I did what every good little captive girl should want to do. I walked out of there in my bare feet with a soft white sheet draped around my naked body, my clothes and confidence long gone. I found a payphone and called 911. I fell asleep curled up beside a Dumpster before help arrived.

Chapter Twelve

FOR THREE DAYS I'd woken up on a soft bed that smelled faintly of roses. Not the sickly sweet scent that got passed off as roses in perfumes, but the real earthy smell of rose petals wafting from cotton sheets. But now a sharp chemical tang burned my nostrils. That was the first thing I noticed, with my eyes closed, my mind still sluggish and half-asleep.

The second thing I noticed was the constant drone of noise. No expectant silence. No lilting strains of *La Bohème*. Instead, machinery beeped and voices sounded muffled in the distance. This bed was hard, the sheet rough and paper-thin between my fingers. I opened my eyes, then immediately shut them. The air felt like sandpaper against the surface of my eyes. An irrepressible groan of pain emanated from my chest.

"Shhh," came a voice from my side. "Take it easy."

For a moment, panic beat in my chest. Was it him? Was I still his captive? And if so, I must have done something wrong to end up here instead.

This was punishment.

He'd taken away my only luxuries, the soft bed, his tender touch.

He would hurt me now, he would…

"Samantha." Sharper now. My name spoken in a command pulled me back. And I recognized him.

"Hennessey."

"That's right. You're okay now. Just rest and take it easy. You don't have to get up right now. You don't have to do anything."

My lips felt dry and cracked. I marveled that I could still feel the slight pinch of them where the skin split, considering the resounding ache in my whole body. I'd read once that the lips were one of the most sensitive parts of the body, a high concentration of receptor cells. Maybe that was why Carlos never kissed me. Maybe he'd thought it would tell me too much. A sob escaped me, manic-sounding, helpless.

A warm hand enclosed mine. "Are you in pain?" he asked, a note of concern deepening his voice. "I'll get a nurse."

I squeezed his hand to stop him. "No, stay."

"Don't try to move. Just rest."

Slumping back against the thin pillow, I sighed. "How long?"

"Twenty-four hours. You've been out of it mostly, on the pain meds."

"Mostly?"

When he said nothing, I knew I must have done something embarrassing. I glanced over to find his expression hard, jaw tense. His nostrils flared. Anger. No, scratch that.

Rage.

"Hennessey, look. I know I disobeyed—"

"Don't you dare give me that bullshit. This isn't your fault."

"But if I'd only—"

"The van and its location were compromised. It wouldn't have mattered if you were inside or not."

I considered that. "How *did* they find out where the van was?" Silence again. "Hennessey?"

He blew out a breath. "Jesus. I think Brody might have set you up."

Shock tore through my chest. "What?"

"I'm sorry. He knew you were Laguardia's type. I think he put you on the team to lure him. And he knew the position of the van… He forced us to move early."

The silence filled in the rest. He'd put me on the team to lure Carlos in. I was a bit of cheese in the mousetrap. That part wasn't a surprise, but what came after had been. The spring hadn't gone off like it should have. Instead of being caught, Carlos had caught me instead. He'd stolen me away, like the thief that he was, the criminal.

"Makes sense." My voice sounded flat. "You always knew there was something off about it. Me, on a high profile case. The rookie."

"Shit. I shouldn't have said anything." He ran his hand through his hair, and only then did I notice how ruffled it looked, the dark blond with glints of silver. He must have been messing with his hair a lot to get it in that state. I'd never seen him looking less than polished before now. For that matter, dark circles marred his bloodshot eyes. His white T-shirt and jeans looked hastily thrown on and rumpled. Had he sat in that straight-edged plastic chair the whole twenty-four hours?

I swallowed. "Look, I can't promise I'm going to be normal or happy, but I don't want you to hide anything from me. I'm still your partner. Right?"

"Right," he said, but his eyes were veiled, and we both knew it was a lie. I would have been pulled, officially, as soon I'd been taken. I might get reinstated, but that would only be after Brody signed off on it. Considering this case had just gotten personal with me, I doubted that would happen.

"Do you… Do you want to talk about it, what happened to you?" He grimaced, self-deprecating, as if aware of the awkwardness he exuded. I imagined he'd have been far more comfortable taking a witness statement, or even better, interrogating me. Instead he offered me friendship.

A smile ghosted over my lips. "I must be really bad off if you aren't even pushing for details."

"Those can wait," he said. Then paused. "I can put Brody off for a few days at least."

I raised my eyebrow. "How, exactly?"

"I'll say you lost your memory. Temporary amnesia."

Reluctantly, I laughed. There was no way in hell Brody would buy that.

"Or we just won't tell him you've woken up. You're

in a coma."

I rolled my eyes, shocked and pleased that we could joke about this. About anything. The awkwardness slipped away, leaving only raw friendship. As if I'd never even left.

"I'm sure he has a direct line to the doctor."

"Then I'll barricade the door and keep him out."

"Held captive again? Out of the frying pan and into the fire."

"Only this time you'd want to stay captive."

My smile slipped. Had I wanted to stay kidnapped before too? I wasn't sure. Any sane person wouldn't, but then I'd figured out a long time ago I wasn't sane.

As a kid, I hadn't wanted my father to hurt me. But I'd resented him that he hadn't. So which was it? Which did I want? Both had pain, one physical, one emotional. Both were sick in their own dark way. It was the only life I knew, one drilled into me as a child. Every moment was defined in terms of pain or its lack. At least pain meant attention.

It meant love.

"What happened at the warehouse? Over the comm, we heard you... It sounded like..."

I couldn't say it. That was how head over heels I was for him—even laid out in a hospital bed, beaten and bruised, I couldn't fathom the idea of him hurt.

His eyes were a million miles deep, just then. He took down the walls and let me see how much it meant to him.

"Laguardia broke free," he said simply.

And yes, it was easy for me to understand how, now that I'd met him. Even without the specifics of what lock and which guard and how so—I knew he wasn't a man to be contained. He was a giant, and not even a hundred little men and all the rope in the world could keep him tethered to the ground.

My voice roughened. "Did you... Did you find him? After?"

After I was recovered.

These images were somehow just as bad as the ones of Hennessey injured had been. I imagined Carlos in handcuffs and an orange jumpsuit. I imagined him dead in a standoff that hadn't ended well. Hennessey's eyes were troubled. The glimmer in his expression clenched a cold fist around my heart. He was unshakeable, but here, now, at the thought of telling me this, he felt something. Gladness that the man he hunted had been caught?

"By the time we followed your tracks to the warehouse, it had been destroyed. We found blood and other...matter at the scene. They're running the DNA at the lab, but we suspect it's Laguardia."

I'd been made of glass, I realized, solid but frail. And now the glass cracked down the middle, branching out into a thousand tiny shards. Carlos, dead or alive. I shouldn't care. I didn't. Either way, I would never see him again. Never get to ask the questions about why he'd taken me or what it all had meant.

They wouldn't find only his DNA. Mine too. Mixed

together and charred in an explosion. Who had set it? Didn't matter. In-fighting, that was what Brody had said. Meaningless deaths.

I should be glad that Carlos was dead. Glad he'd never hurt me again. It was completely irrational to wish I could see him again, to imagine him tracking me down at the hospital or later. To wish he would abduct me again. Even now, I shook with fear and anticipation.

God, I was crazy. Imagining a bad guy, even when I knew he was dead.

Hennessey's voice roughened. "I'm sorry we couldn't catch him. Couldn't…bring him to justice."

Justice. "It's okay."

"Jesus, Samantha." He scrubbed a hand over his face. "Three days…"

Three days, and with every passing hour, the chances of surviving had dwindled down to nothing. Like an integral equation, arcing low but never touching the baseline, racing toward zero into infinity. But I'd lived. Coincidence? Hennessey didn't believe in coincidence, and strangely enough, neither did I.

In his steel eyes, I saw bleakness reflected. Had he searched the morgues for Jane Does? Had they run DNA tests on nameless, faceless corpses? I felt sick for him. Sick for myself. I should have been on the slab. Then everyone's lives would be simpler. Just like my father should have murdered me along with all the other kids he hurt. Why did I always have to live?

Survivor's guilt. The textbook hadn't been far off the mark. And it sucked.

Tears slipped down my cheeks, and I clenched my hands.

Hennessey put his hand over my balled fist. "It will be okay. It will...get better."

I shook my head. How could it get better? There would never be any closure, not with my father and not with Carlos. There'd never be any reasoning behind the actions of a psychopath. I should be happy to be safe again, to be in this buzzing, beeping, cold hospital room. I should be glad to have my partner at my side, when I wasn't really even his partner anymore.

But I couldn't be happy. An ineffable sadness weighed me down, heavy as lead, molten as lava.

A single tear slipped down my cheek, like a crack in my skin. A crack in my false composure, and I was lost. Sobs tore from my throat before I could hold them back. They racked my body, rattling the thin metal frame of the hospital bed. I cowered on the sheets, feeling exposed and miserable. Alone. For three stuttering, helpless cries I *was* alone. Then Hennessey scooped me up. He held me in his arms, sitting on the hospital bed while I spilled tears onto his T-shirt, while I breathed his musk and clutched at broad shoulders.

Should have died, should have died.

All I could think was that I wanted to die. But I already had. When Carlos had hurt me, when I'd realized I liked it after all, that even as an adult I still wanted the abuse—it had been a form of death. It felt like dying, but the part that really hurt the most was coming back to life.

CHAPTER THIRTEEN

WHEN I WOKE up a second time, the room was empty. I glanced around, suddenly alert. A rap came at the door, and I managed to croak a weak, "Come in."

The door opened in shadows, and a small frame entered. A stab of disappointment lanced through me. Not Hennessey. But instead of a nurse coming to check on me, like I'd thought, a familiar face emerged.

"Mrs. Martinez," I said in surprise.

She gave me a gently chiding look. "Call me Mia."

I struggled to sit up, but a sharp pain stole my breath away.

Making a *tsking* sound, she rushed to my side. "Lie down, love. Don't strain yourself. Here, let me help you."

Mia eased me back to the thin comfort of the hospital bed and tucked the sheet around my waist. I let her do it...because damn, I ached all over.

I wasn't even sure how I'd really gotten hurt. I winced as the harsh sheets pressed against my back, but that was a small twinge compared to the overall pain in my body. It felt like I'd been beaten—not beaten with a whip or a leather strap, but beaten with fists and kicks inside my body. But when I ran my hands over my stomach, I didn't feel any bruises or cuts. The pain was on the inside, hurt and anger coalescing into a sick burn inside me.

Mia's expression was pure sympathy. No, scratch that. Empathy. Like she knew exactly what I was going through. Which she did, really. She'd been with Carlos. I tried to let that sink in. She'd been through exactly what I'd been through, except instead of days, she'd been with him for *years*.

"How did you do it?" I asked helplessly.

Her smile was sad. "It was hard sometimes. Other times…I found it surprisingly easy. To put my trust in someone who was strong enough to take it. To focus on the sensations only. But I'd been with him a long time by then. I wouldn't expect it to be the same for you."

Her voice lilted up at the last word, turning it into a question. The really crazy part was that I understood what she was saying. The release of being bound and gagged, the freedom of having nowhere else to go. And instead of feeling horror, I felt curiosity. Was he always that rigid in the way that he fucked her? Was he relentlessly cruel? Or had he, at some point, opened up to her?

Strangely enough, that had hurt the most. If he had been a mindless, heartless animal and treated me that way, I could have understood it. I could have moved past it. You didn't blame an animal for biting you. A monster only knew how to scare. But Carlos had too much intelligence, too much *thoughtfulness* to his actions to be an animal. A monster. He was just a person. He wasn't kind, but then neither was the world.

"I hope you don't mind me coming here," Mia said. "I can go if you're too tired…or if seeing me will upset you."

"No, I'd like to talk to you. Actually," I said, feeling unaccountably shy, "I'd like it if you could talk to me. Tell me about your time with him. We didn't get to talk very long the day I came to see you. And now I—" I spread my palms, as if in supplication. I wasn't sure what I wanted to know or why. Only that she was part of the answer.

She drew up the plastic chair and sat down. "I can tell you about him. Maybe it will help you reconcile what happened. Or…I don't know, help with closure."

"Or help us catch him," I whispered.

"Right. Of course." She said it so quickly that she clearly didn't think it would happen. To her, he was invincible. And I wasn't sure she was wrong.

I sighed, letting my eyes fall closed. In the darkened hospital room, it was almost the same. My eyes felt tired, and I let her words wash over me like a lullaby. Like a story before bedtime, and that was what it was. Her voice was a sweet melody, soothing to my roughened nerves.

"Carlos's father ran a fairly large drug trafficking operation out of Colombia. His mother was an American woman. I saw a picture of her once. She was really beautiful. Exquisite. And you couldn't tell her origins from the picture. Her dress was shimmery, and she had diamond earrings and a necklace. It was kind of a fairy tale, back then, and they were royalty."

I could picture them, the stern-faced drug lord in a sharp suit. The glittering bride at his side, elegant and severe. My mind painted them in black and white, with vintage glamour. But this story had a dark side. Even light casts a shadow.

"Families were important back then. All the important men had wives and kids and they'd meet up for big dinners. *La familia*." Mia's laugh sounded soft and musical, like a wind chime in the night air. "When Carlos was eight years old, there was a dinner. His parents' anniversary and it was a big affair. But the two of them had been fighting that day, in private. The way things worked, the women didn't talk back to the men. Not ever."

Mia paused, and I felt her sadness drench the air. For who, though? For Carlos? Or for the woman from a previous generation, who was so much like her. Used for her body and elevated through her status with a man who did her harm.

"That night, she turned on him. In front of everyone, she shouted at him and told him she'd been sneaking behind his back. He pulled out his gun and shot her. In front of Carlos."

I shivered in horror and sympathy, imagining that moment. Remembering how it felt to see violence too young and unprepared. None of this excused what Carlos had done, but I could tell from Mia's voice that she knew that too. More than that, I got the sense she hadn't even thought he'd done wrong. We were all animals, acting on instinct. He was just a particularly intelligent and powerful animal. A lion with rippling muscles and a beautiful mane and a pair of jaws that could rip you to shreds if he wanted.

"He kept the party going. That was the breaking point for Carlos, I think. They removed the body, and his father kept the party going because they already had everyone there, and food, and music."

"That's awful," I whispered, feeling the horror of it wash over me. Imagining a little boy, who had probably already seen too much, being told to pretend that nothing had happened. That his mother hadn't just died.

Mia nodded. "He went to live with relatives after that, and he barely ever saw his father. They were involved in the organization as well, so he still saw what was happening, but he had no plans to follow in his footsteps. In fact, he…"

She trailed off, and I looked at her. Her smile was wistful. "He had other life plans."

"What were they?"

"I don't know," she said, but that was a lie. She knew. It was just weird that after telling me all this personal stuff about Carlos, she'd omit something like this. Surely it wouldn't matter if he'd wanted to be a doctor or even a racecar driver or whatever little boys wanted to be.

"Go on," I murmured, determined to get as much information—honest information—from her as I could.

She lifted one slender shoulder. "He told me when he picked me up off the street, when he decided to keep me...he said he was going to shoot me one day. So don't get too comfortable. At the time I believed him."

I remembered her using the same phrase at our last meeting. "At the time. And what do you think now?"

"I learned to trust him by his actions, not what he said."

"So he didn't put you in chains? He didn't whip you?" I demanded, already knowing the answer.

"He did." She nodded. "But he always took care of me after. That's not what you do if you don't care. Believe me. I met plenty of men who wouldn't have. But Carlos didn't let them touch me...until the end. When things started breaking down."

"Why did he let you go?"

Her eyes were open, guileless. A deep, bottomless brown. "I think he started to care about me, honestly. More than he was comfortable with. He started to worry that he *would* shoot me. That he'd marry me and care about me, and that he'd act on instinct. On blood. It's not entirely logical, but when horrible things happen to young children, they change the way they think."

A shiver ran through me. A premonition? I knew exactly how much the horrific events of a young child could shape a life. My brain had been wired different from everyone else's at that young, impressionable age. I hadn't realized how lonely it made me. But Carlos knew what it felt like. And so did Mia, both because she had experienced it herself and because she had an innate compassion that bled through her every word. I began to understand why Carlos had kept her for so long, and it wasn't only for her lithe body or delicate features.

"He told you all this?"

She must have heard the disbelief in my voice. Her smile was wry. "Not at first. He tried to keep things really strict. Completely separate. But he must have realized he could trust me. He started opening up to me. About his hopes. His fears."

I could have laughed. I didn't. "His fears? What would that be, not making enough of a profit on the illegal drugs he's importing?"

"Something like that. You see, when his father died, the empire he had built would have passed down to Carlos. Except Carlos didn't want to have anything to do with it. He was done."

This caught my attention. "What happened?'

"There was a second in command. An older man, closer to Carlos's father's age. He assumed control, and that would have been the end of it. But he didn't trust Carlos. I don't know whether he thought Carlos would rat them out, since he knew so much, or if he thought Carlos would come back looking for a piece of the pie. So he decided to have Carlos killed. Sent a couple guys on a hit."

My palms were sweating. My heart pounded, as if I cared. Silly, because obviously Carlos had made it through alive, but something in me still yearned to hear the completion. To know that he'd made it out okay. It was as if he'd tied us together somehow, merged a part of our bodies so that now his safety was mine. His happiness too. Disturbing, considering he was a sadist and a psychopath.

"Carlos killed them. I believe they were the first lives he ever took. Self-defense."

Yes, it would have been self-defense. If he'd gone directly to the police and explained the situation. But if he'd done that, he would have been a sitting duck for the next pair of hit men who came along. Without even hearing the words, I knew Carlos had done the only thing he could do. He survived. And as fucked up as it was, I respected that. There was no good or bad, sometimes. There was just living and not living. A person had a right to do whatever it took to survive.

I had to believe that, otherwise my actions at the warehouse were untenable.

Self-defense.

"He knew more men would be after him, so he went after the guy in charge directly. Killed him and replaced him as the head of the organization. But there was chaos by then. Losing their leader twice. Having a young man in charge of everything, one who didn't even want to be there. People started flipping out. There were so many deaths. It was chaos, and Carlos was sucked into it, righting the organization and bringing everything back to order."

"Why didn't he just turn them in?" The question was out before I could call it back. I'd just meant that he could be free of the situation, wash his hands of the heritage he'd never wanted.

"They were family," she said simply.

And yes, of course. Because normal people didn't sell out their family. That was only for the disloyal, like me. How dare I call Carlos cruel when he hadn't been able to do what I did, turn my back on blood.

✧ ✧ ✧

"What do you remember?"

The psychologist sat with her legs crossed in a short pencil skirt. Did she know how much attention she drew to them? Did she want her male patients to look at her legs? Fucking psychologists. Voyeurs and exhibitionists.

Her question hung in the air. What did I remember about my captivity, she meant. But the question was open ended, and I wasn't thinking about captivity. New memories had started to float to the surface, ones long repressed.

A better question would have been: *How did you escape your father's attention?*

No one has ever hurt me. It had been my mantra for so long, a lament and longing rolled into one. But was it true? I could no longer be sure. Of that, of anything.

"Samantha?" she prodded.

"I don't remember. It's all a blank." It wasn't completely a lie. It wasn't blank, but it was a blur.

Her eyebrows rose. "You don't remember anything?"

"I remember Lance. He's one of the agents I work with. I remember we were stepping out of the van, trying to figure out what had happened. Everyone inside the warehouse had gone quiet."

"Were you worried?" she asked.

She was trying to profile *me*. And doing a piss poor job of it, too. But I was a good little agent, so I answered. "Yes. The plan was very specific. And we'd heard them over the comm. Something was wrong."

"What did you do then?"

"We headed toward the location to see if we could help. Only, we got separated. And…someone attacked me. They disarmed me before I could stop them. I remember being punctured with a needle. Some kind of drug."

I looked at her, the nameless, faceless woman who was supposed to analyze me. She'd be the one signing off on my return to duty. Her expression was politely blank. Her eyes were placid—borderline vacant. The only reason I knew she was listening was her pencil moving, marking down notes, judging me.

"And that's it," I finished.

"You never got a good look at him?"

"No," I said, and at least that much was honest. "I

never got a good look at him."

The master of disguise and evasion. He could have been anyone. He could have been any man I passed on the street, and I wouldn't even know it. And wasn't that the fucking tragedy.

CHAPTER FOURTEEN

"HELL NO," LANCE said over the phone.

"Please."

He swore. "I can't believe you're still hung up on Hennessey after..."

"After getting raped?"

"I just would have thought you didn't want company. Not that way."

Yeah, I would have thought that too. Instead, I felt the opposite. Whereas before I had been satisfied with steamy moments and hot kisses, they were no longer enough. They were too weak to counter the memory of handcuffs and whips, of hard phallic objects inside me. The memory of pain. I wanted something more, *needed* the closure pleasure could give me. That Hennessey could give me.

"Never mind," I told Lance. "I'll find it another way."

He swore again, low and vicious. "Fine. I'll get it for you. But you know he's just going to drop you as soon as he gets a new assignment. Don't come crying to me when he does."

"Okay. And Lance?"

"Yeah?"

"Thank you."

It took him an hour to find out where Hennessey was staying by pulling his credit card receipts, and then I was on the road. He didn't live too far from me, but this being Houston, that meant a thirty-minute drive time. The streets were mostly empty this late at night, with only the streetlights to guide me, like candles left in the window. For all I knew he wouldn't even be home. And even if he were, he might not want me. Like Lance said, I was a passing interest for him. The rookie he could kiss in the supply closet for a little mutual stress relief. That was okay. I thought of the future differently now. It wasn't about reaching toward some picturesque future with dinner dates and presents at Christmas. I couldn't ever be that normal, and I had more pressing goals at the moment. It was about survival, body and soul. My soul needed this.

The hotel was in Montrose, quaint and built for extended stays, like an apartment with housekeeping service. The office was dark, appearing closed. I circled around back counting the numbers on the doors until I found the one Lance had told me. This was it. The phrase *do or die* had never felt more real to me than now.

I knocked on the door.

A minute later, Hennessey opened it. He covered his surprise quickly, leaning on the door and blocking the entrance. His bare chest gleamed, the sprinkling of hairs silvery in the moonlight. Drawstring pants hung low on his waist, revealing angled hipbones and a V-shape that drew my eyes down. My gaze skated over the bulge visible through the thin fabric and down to his bare feet. He was casual. Sensual. Perfect.

"How did you find me?" he asked, raising an eyebrow.

I flashed back to when he'd shown up at my apartment. "FBI Agent."

"Stalker."

My voice came out husky. "I come bearing gifts."

His gaze dropped to the jacket I wore. A plain trench coat that ended at my knees. Not dirty in the slightest, except for the red heels I'd paired with it. They sent a different message. They hinted there was nothing underneath the coat, except maybe a few scraps of lace. They hinted at a present waiting to be unwrapped.

A muscle in his jaw ticked. His eyes stared at some point beyond my shoulder. I expected him to protest. *You're only doing this because you were damaged.* Even a token protest seemed likely. I only hoped he wouldn't turn me away completely. He had to know I was only here because I needed to be.

"Forgiven," he finally said, stepping back to let me in.

I sighed in relief that he wasn't going to fight this, fight me. Maybe getting beaten and violated should have already broken me, but they hadn't. I'd wanted to know how it felt for so long; the anticipation had been a form of preparation.

The reality had been more and less than I had expected. More, because everything hurt worse and cut deeper than I could have imagined. I'd received bland disinterest from my foster parents and rote chivalry from the men I had dated. It had been like living in a world of black and white, like having that world slashed with red. Beautiful and alarming.

The experience had also meant less, because I never understood why Laguardia had taken me. I only skated the surface with him, so distanced by metal and leather and glass and every other type of material he'd used between our bodies. Whips and restraints and dildos had formed a barrier between us. That was *why* he'd used them. But that hadn't been fair to me. I was left with half an obsession, one side of the deviant coin. Now I needed to reach out and touch someone. I needed to *be* touched.

Hennessey remained by the door while I strolled around the room. He might have been a guard, a lock and key, if it weren't for the troubled light in his eyes. I saw everything in terms of captivity now, in the cold continuum between freedom and pain. Neither had ever fulfilled me.

"Samantha." The word was laden with questions, bending under their weight. Why I was here and what I wanted. Whether or not I was okay.

Who knew, really? Getting abducted might have broken my sanity. Or finding out my father was a serial killer. Or falling in love with my partner, a man who would never really respect me and never stick around.

Any one of those was enough to drive me crazy, so what did it matter which one had pulled the trigger? If there was one certain victim in all this, it was my sanity.

My hands went to my belt. I untied the knot and held the sides of my coat together. I had to give him fair warning, so he could blot out the shock and pity from his eyes.

"There's still some bruising."

Something flickered in his eyes, but his expression remained stoic. "I see," he said quietly.

He didn't see. He couldn't. I opened the coat and let it fall, closing my eyes at the sound of his stuttered breath. My front had mostly healed. Carlos had gone easier here, though I hadn't realized it at the time. There were only a few lingering marks and some yellowish bruising. I looked like I'd been spray painted gold, uneven and whimsical. In the dim light of the lamp, the effect probably faded to a mere glimmer.

I turned, and felt the impact of my back hit him with resounding, utter silence. There was no pretty frame of mind I could put around red slashes and blue-black bruises. Perversely, it looked worse now than it had felt at the time. I'd gone into a kind of cloud-like space, floated away on endorphins and fear until the pain looked blurry and dark, like the earth beneath an airplane.

However it had felt then, it looked awful now. I'd stared at the marks in the mirror, looking over my shoulder. He'd turned me into some sort of abstract painting, something that could hang on a metropolitan museum with the title "A Dark Love" written on a little white placard. It was the most angry, meaningful, caring thing any person had ever done to me, but I could never tell Hennessey that. He wouldn't understand. It was just another secret to take to my grave.

"Do you still want me?" I wouldn't blame him for turning me away.

The air stirred behind me. I felt his heat at my back.

He dropped a kiss on my bare shoulder. "This was done to you. It wasn't your fault. You know that. Don't you?"

I shook my head. A lump formed in my throat, barring any words. But that was just as well. What I had to say couldn't fit into the accepted language of a woman. *A survivor not a victim*, they said. As if the word mattered, when I could feel the lingering wounds with every breath I took. They may have been done to me, but they were a part of me now. Taken into my skin, my soul. My outside finally matched what was inside—that was the gift Carlos gave me.

Hennessey ran his fingers down my arms, feather light. "Let me in," he murmured. "Let me in."

I knew what he wanted. To take care of me, to comfort me. To control me. The same thing Carlos had wanted. They weren't so different, and with a sigh, I closed my eyes and sank into him. My head rested on his chest, cradled by the hard muscles of a man who worked more than he rested.

His musk enveloped me like a lullaby. *Put your fears to sleep.* And in his arms, I found acceptance for my outward hideousness, if not the inside. He pressed kisses along my temple and down my hairline. He kissed the skin below my ear and continued until he found the seam of my neck and my shoulder. A sensitive place, one smooth and free of any bruises or whip marks.

"You're beautiful," he murmured.

I had to close my eyes, because he didn't know. Didn't really see me. I wanted to blurt it out, suddenly, when keeping the secret had been my entire life's work. I'd gone to see therapists and entered the academy, constantly moving, striving, running away from the truth. No one had ever hurt me, but that was a lie I told myself.

Turning in his arms, I faced him. The unadulterated sorrow in his face struck me like a lash. I'd done this to him, some way and somehow, and I was about to make it worse. The hotel's A/C rained down cold air, raising goose bumps on my flesh. I was naked, brutally so. It was fitting, because I felt so exposed. Raw. Split open. Primed for a confession I'd barely even acknowledged to myself.

"I turned my father in. For murder. For rape. A bunch of other charges."

"I know," he said simply.

"He's there for life. I don't really know how he escaped the death penalty."

"You did the right thing."

"Did I?" I laughed and the sound was hollow. "My own father. My own flesh and blood. How can you trust me if I'd turn on my own family?"

"I trust you."

I shook my head. He didn't understand. "I didn't turn him in because I just figured out he had killed someone. I suspected all along."

His expression didn't change. "You were a child."

"Yes. A child."

I closed my eyes as the truth flayed me open, more brutally than Carlos's whip had ever done. *What do you remember?* I remembered my father hurting me, and every time I'd told myself he hadn't, it had been a lie.

"He molested me from the time I was six years old."

Hennessey sucked in a breath. I felt his shock. I felt *my* shock, at the truth I'd barely acknowledged in my own mind.

This will be our little secret, okay?

This was what my father had meant. Not the murders, the other children that he'd thought were a secret anyway. He'd meant his abuse of me. That would be our little secret, and until this moment, I'd never told anyone. How obedient. I'd never even admitted it to myself.

I kept going. Couldn't stop now. "Until I was eight. Then I guess I was too old for him. I don't know. He just stopped coming. And you know what the crazy part is?"

He did know. I could see the painful knowledge in

his eyes. He would have studied enough victim psychology to understand how the mind works, especially one so young.

"I missed it," I whispered. "I missed him coming to see me. Even though it hurt. Even though I knew it was wrong. How fucked up is that?"

"You were a child," he repeated, more forcefully. His jaw was clenched. His whole body vibrated with anger, with energy, but I felt just the opposite, strangely deflated. I had almost, *almost* been able to keep this a secret from myself. If I just didn't *think* about it, I didn't have to know the truth.

"That's why I told on him. To punish him for going to other children instead of me. I knew...I knew other kids were getting hurt, but I said nothing. Not until I was *jealous*." I spat the final word, disgusted with myself. Bitterness thickened my voice. "He knew, too. My dad. That was what he said to me the last time I saw him. In jail. 'I should've killed you too.'"

In the span of a second, Hennessey grabbed me. Crushed me against his chest, his arms hurting, his chest comforting. Oh God. I was so fucking crazy. He was never going to want to be with me now. I'd lost more than just my fake sanity. I'd lost *him*.

Still, I closed my eyes and let him hold me. I pretended he'd stay with me after this. I pretended he wouldn't tell the Bureau I couldn't work there anymore because I was insane and awful and broken inside. It would be a relief, in a way, for everyone to finally see the monster within. A relief to admit it to myself.

Every time I'd dreamed of someone hurting me, it hadn't been because I didn't know how it would feel. It was because I *did* know how it felt, and I wanted to have it again. The fear and the pain. It had become a drug for me in my formative years, and the addiction had never gone away. Never would.

I'd pretended to be normal for years, wished for it, but even as I stood in front of a man who could give that to me, I'd ruined it. A man who had built his career, his *life* around putting people in jail wouldn't want a woman who had let a criminal go unchecked for so long. Being a child didn't excuse me. Being a victim didn't either. But just for tonight, I wanted to pretend. Another form of lying, but it was all I had left.

I moved against him, the slightest undulation to change the shape of our embrace. My breasts were already against his chest, tucked between my arms, and I rubbed them on him like a cat, marking him with my scent.

Turning my head, I kissed his chest, reveling in the coarse hairs that tickled my lips. He was strong where I was soft, rough where I was smooth. Distilled into the essence of masculinity and reformed in my arms, hard and pulsing. I wanted to hold him like this forever, to map every hollow and callus on his body, but there wasn't time for that. This wasn't a leisurely exploration; it was an invasion, quick and fierce, before he changed his mind. I placed open-mouthed kisses on his nipple.

He jerked against me.

"Samantha, we don't have to do this." His voice sounded strained, on a razor thin edge.

I glanced down at the bulge, its shape and girth clearly visible beneath the thin fabric of his pants. "But you want to."

His eyes flashed. "I've always wanted to."

But he wouldn't. First because I was his partner. And now? Because I'd been hurt, beaten. Normal men didn't want to fuck a woman like that. I was too broken for rough sex, wasn't I? If anything, they could make love or cuddle or… No. I didn't want some diluted version of him. I might be broken, but that didn't mean I wanted him to hide the worst of him. I craved the worst of him.

"Please," I begged. "Carlos…he took something from me. Let me do this with you. Be normal."

He sighed. "This isn't normal, Samantha. It's messed up."

"I'm messed up!" I shouted, angry now. "What the hell else am I going to do?"

Silence. His expression was pained.

All I could do was push and push. And all he could do was take it. "Should I go on match.com? Do I mention my recent run-in with torture and rape in the bio section or wait until the first date to tell them?"

"*Jesus.*"

"Well, what do you want me to say? No one wants someone fucked up and broken. You don't either. So where does that leave me? Should I go find someone like

Carlos? At least they'll still fuck me."

He looked fit to strangle someone. Me, probably. His expression was molten lava, burning hot and terrifying. Excitement thrummed through me. I wanted this. Pure emotion, unfiltered.

What do you remember?

I wanted to remember this.

CHAPTER FIFTEEN

"**G**ET ON THE bed," he said.

A tremor ran through me. Fear? Desire? I couldn't tell the difference anymore.

"Get on the fucking bed." His voice sharpened, but even now, I wasn't sure he would actually go through with it. Maybe he'd tuck me in and leave me here, as if I really had died under Carlos's hand. As if I'd died when my father should have killed me. All my life, trying to see if I was even still alive.

But I went. I lay down on the bed, and he followed, standing beside me. There was no place to hide, spread out on cool sheets. He stared down at the silvery lash marks on my breasts and swallowed. Did they disgust him? He bent and placed a kiss on my nipple. I shut my eyes. Another kiss landed on a half-healed bruise, and I flinched.

"Does it hurt?" he asked hoarsely.

I shook my head. He licked a cut with barely-formed scar tissue, and despite bracing myself, I whimpered.

He made a sound of regret. "Don't lie to me."

"I don't..." I opened my eyes. He looked down at me, curious and heartbroken. "It hurts, but I don't want you to stop." *I don't want you to leave me.*

His frown was uncertain. He had to know how fucked up all this was, but he'd straddled the world of the criminal and the law-abiding for so long, he knew also how little that mattered in the end. Sane and crazy. Right and wrong. It all whirred together like the tinsel-bright colors of a carousel going round and round. Here. Now. That was all we had.

Slow, so I'd have time to stop him, he bent to kiss another cut. Another bruise. He licked and nuzzled and caressed every point of pain on my breasts. He moved down my belly, which was mostly bare. My thighs were marked more deeply than my breasts had been. It was a testament to Carlos's care of me that the severity of the wounds depended on the place. He hadn't been randomly beating me. He'd been careful, giving me only as much as I could take. And my thighs could take a lot, judging from the slash marks I'd seen in the mirror. The ones Hennessey stared at now. What did he feel? Disgust?

He did the same for them, licking and kissing until my hips rolled up in silent invitation. *Please, here.* He did move to my center, licking at my cunt with skill and eagerness. But only on my outer lips. He nudged my hip, and following his tacit instructions, I turned over. He repeated the strange healing process starting at the nape of my neck. He trailed his tongue along a thinly formed scab on a cut, and I gasped. He sucked at a bruise, sending sparks of pain to my core. The sensations were tied up between surface pain and deep, sensual pleasure. They were tied up between natural aversion and a childhood longing.

He worked his way down my body, over the valley of my lower back and the hills of my ass. Lower still, until he reached my ankles and circled them lightly where the chains had been. I jerked when I felt something soft and wet at the bottom of my feet, right on the heel. He kissed and licked there too. It felt strange at first, as if he were abasing himself—and I would never ask that of him. But it was different when given freely, like he did for me now. Where once I'd felt the worst kind of pain imaginable for fleeting, heart-stopping seconds, now he caressed the tender skin with his lips, laved it with his tongue. He found each wound on my body and he loved it—and in that way I found the acceptance I'd been searching for. Carlos had hurt me, but that was only one half of the equation. But this, this was the answer.

A cell phone rang in the distance, but he muttered for me to ignore it. As if to ensure his command, he pulled my hips up, so I knelt on the bed face down. It was wholly undignified the way my face and breasts hugged the sheets and my ass pointed at the ceiling. Wholly undignified the way he pressed his face between my legs from behind, licking and sucking at my cunt. He delved deeper this time, lapping at the moisture in my core, drawing it out.

He found my clit and circled it, pressing the flat of his tongue against it in a timeless rhythm until I moaned against the sheets and warm liquid dripped down the inside of my thigh. He made love to me with his mouth, moving over every place that Carlos had touched, that Carlos had *hurt*.

Hennessey's touch didn't erase the pain. He made it sharper. Sweeter. I still felt the ache, jerking and crying out at the touch of wet tongue to torn skin. He saw the darkness written on my skin, and he wanted me anyway. The thought spurred me higher, on the roughened currents of hope.

I pushed back against him, shoving my wet cunt against his face, begging him to take more of me, all of it. Fingers slipped inside me, filling me where I needed him. It wasn't enough though, and I clenched around him with my secret muscles, begging for reprieve only he could give me.

He pushed my hips down flat on the bed and placed his cock at my entrance.

"Tell me it's okay," he said.

He had to know I wanted him, from the dampness drenching the crown of his cock to my breathless moans urging him on. He knew, but he wanted me to state it clearly, unequivocally. That was the difference between him and Carlos. Carlos had reveled in my lack of consent, had gotten off on it. This man wanted more than my reluctant participation. He wanted my full-fledged desire, and he had it. I wanted his strong body. His intelligent mind. His unrelenting sense of honor. I wanted all of him.

"Yes. Please. Take me."

"More," he said on a groan.

I begged. "God, please. I want to feel you inside me. I need to… Let me…"

My words ended on a gasp and a sudden sense of fullness. I couldn't breathe. Could only gasp against the bed, sucking the fabric against my lips and muffling the sound of my pain. I was still sore here, something I hadn't known about before coming here. I didn't regret it; like his kisses before, his touch on the bruises left behind made everything richer. Layers of pleasure on pain, an indulgence of sensation. I gripped him with my cunt, and he pulsed inside me, a shared and private communion I could feel and observe but not change. Along for the ride as he picked up his pace, pushing inside me faster and deeper, finding a spot that made me gush all over his cock and down my legs.

"Feel me," he grunted. "Feel me." It became a chant, muttered under his breath, indistinguishable from his rough, needy sounds.

I knew exactly what he meant. More than touch, more than words. He wanted to leave his mark some-where deeper, but he'd already done so. Before I'd even been captured, I'd fallen for him. What we did now just retraced those lines on my body, over my heart.

The pressure built and tightened through my body, centering around the invasion of his cock, exploding over me and raining down sparks I felt in every cut, in every bruise. I moaned against the sheets, out of breath and mindless, giving myself over to the utter weightlessness of hope and the breadth of desire. Open, trusting. Finding exactly what I needed around the pulsing hotness of his erection. He stiffened behind me as he rocked against my ass, the sound of his low groan filling me and sinking deep into my core.

There wasn't any place to hide as his body sank down on mine. Not any way to lie to myself about how much I wanted him like this, sated and spent, bonded and broken. The feeling seemed to be mutual. He let out a quiet sigh, acceptance and need wrapped into one.

✧   ✧   ✧

THE ACCEPTANCE WAS too much, too complete. I couldn't believe in it, especially when I'd only just admitted the full extent of my father's abuse to myself. I tried to warn him about the poison inside me—the shame and the guilt. To protect him. From me.

"Do you remember the story," I whispered in the dark, "of the scorpion and the frog? The frog carried the scorpion on its back as they crossed the river. The scorpion stung the frog, and as they both were drowning, the frog asked the scorpion why he'd done it."

"Because I'm a scorpion," he finished.

I stayed silent, my point made.

He made a small sound, a puff of air, incredulous. "*You* are not the scorpion."

"But—"

"You're not. Now *shh*. Come here."

And he proceeded to make me forget I'd ever doubted. We made love countless times over the course of the night. Each time I woke with hands on my body and his cock deep inside me. I'd opened a dam, and he rushed forward, poured forth, unstoppable in his passion. And I received him, made myself a vessel to hold whatever he gave me.

As yellow light filtered through the waffle-patterned curtains, I grew to trust in what he offered me. It wasn't forever. Even better, it was now. He was used to dealing with some of the toughest criminals in the world. And sure, he wasn't trying to date them. But the point was, he didn't fear me. Not what had happened to me as a child or what had happened with Carlos. I didn't need to warn him away any longer. He understood. He stayed.

At least until I woke the final time. I stretched and felt...nothing. Just a warm spot where he had been. I could hear the shower running. I could imagine him naked with water running down his body, winding its way over his skin like a liquid web, catching him for me. That made me the spider. I was the cautionary tale, but he'd always been a risk taker. Tackling the toughest cases at the FBI. He didn't feel fear like normal people, which made him perfect for a girl who'd been afraid her whole life.

In the bright morning light, I couldn't quite believe I'd confessed to him about my father. It felt like a dream, but then everything related to my father felt that way. The memories of him coming into my room. Repressed memories. I sighed. A psychologist would have a field day with that one, but I was done with that. It hadn't fixed me. Nothing could.

I'd seen a tree once with an indent running all the way around the trunk. Something had been there and the tree had grown around it, damaged but still alive. That was me. I was as healthy as I could be all on my own. As for the Bureau, I'd see one of their psychologists to get cleared for duty, but I wasn't going to bare my soul. I had a meeting with Brody today. I wondered if he'd give me the results of the psych exam. There were mandatory minimums for things like this, but as long as no red flags came up in the therapy sessions, Brody would have to reinstate me. I just had to wait them out, and with Hennessey in my home, it was no hardship.

Water rushed in a soothing rhythm. His golden skin would glisten. His hands would roam over himself, soapy and brisk. He would clean that lovely cock, wash our scent from the roll of skin. I wanted to taste him freshly washed. To feel the satiny head of his cock against my tongue, tasteless and wet. It would be a morning gift to him and to myself. I pressed my face against his pillow and breathed in deep. Musk. Man. And so familiar. Only one night and I could scent him like an animal. Like a mate.

I slipped from the bed, feeling twinges from my body. I felt deliciously sore, aching in the places well-used and throbbing for more in another. I padded across the thin carpet to the bathroom door and stopped.

Humming.

That was what I noticed first, the humming from inside. I thought it was sweet and endearing. Then why did my blood chill? But it did. I tried to place the song but my mind eluded me, running away before I could be sure. *You don't want to know,* it promised. But too late, too late I realized what it was. The haunting refrains of *La Bohème*. A chill raced over my bare skin.

I stood outside the door clutching my stomach. It had to be a coincidence. A famous classical opera with iconic music. Anyone could know the piece. Anyone could hum in the shower, without realizing it would trigger hateful memories. Though did I really hate what had happened to me? Or did I just think that was the right response? Always pretending, always lying, so much I hardly knew which way was up.

Remembrance sliced through my wounds. The pain of the whip. The humiliation of being fucked with leather and with glass.

The hopelessness of being captive to a stranger.

Except he hadn't been a stranger, had he? A laugh escaped me, and it sounded maniacal. Last night, Hennessey had flicked at my clit in time with the music. It had soothed me, so much warmer than when the leather flogger had done the same. Except how had Hennessey known to do it? He'd kissed the soles of my feet, except they'd had no bruises in the hospital. I'd never shared that detail in the debriefings afterward. So how had he known I'd been hurt there?

Because he is Carlos.

No. That's crazy. *You're crazy,* I told myself. But the truth of the statement remained. I knew it because he sang *La Bohème* in the shower. I knew it because he made love to me with his mouth the same way he'd once done with leather. And most of all, I knew it because I recognized the darkness in him. I'd always feared that part of him, from that first interview in prison when I'd suspected Hennessey was capable of worse things than I knew. Had I known all along? Had I suspected?

I wasn't sure, but I knew now. I felt scared, suddenly. I felt cold, deep inside. I felt as hollow as a drum, and he just beat and beat and beat me.

The room closed in on me, shrinking. I dressed quickly. Easy, considering all I had were my heels and a trench coat. My hair and face were a mess, but I couldn't care about that. Outside the hotel room door, I walked quickly to my car, half expecting Hennessey to come running out, demanding to know where I was going. Or would it be Carlos who emerged from the shower, ready to take over where the kinder man had left off? Dr. Jekyll. Mr. Hyde. They could both go fuck themselves.

At home, I ran straight to the bathroom and threw up. There wasn't much in my stomach, thank God. Foamy residue floated on top of the toilet water. My stomach heaved again, and I gagged, open-mouthed and dry over the seat. I slumped against the wall with my eyes closed.

My mouth was dry and acidic, but I could still taste

the fear. Harsh. Bitter. A sickening sense of inevitability sank in my stomach. It was like I'd always been reaching toward this moment. As if I'd always end up here, facing the same dilemma that had haunted me my whole life.

Should I tell on my father? Which was more important, the lives of strangers or the life of the only person in the world who gave a shit about me? Selfish. I'd been selfish and at eight years old, maybe that was excusable. And now? The same choice. Carlos deserved to be behind bars. He deserved the death penalty, not only for punishment of past deeds, but to protect any people he might hurt in the future. But Hennessey was the only man I'd ever wanted a future with. The only man who might see me, underneath the hopeful façade and to the darkness beneath, and still want me.

I could hear the clock ticking down the minutes in my head, a barely breathing time bomb. I'd have to decide soon. My meeting with Brody was today. That was the time to tell him. I couldn't wait and see Hennessey again. My expression would give me away, and then he'd have to...what? Would he kill me for figuring out his secret? He'd have to, to keep himself safe. It would be self-defense for him.

Self-defense? My laugh came out rough, my throat still raw. I could rationalize anything, even my own murder. It was a twisted sort of love, but it was the only kind I knew.

People professed that their love was unconditional, but it wasn't really. What if someone did something awful? Like murder or rape or organizing major weapons deals across nations? The love would end. *I didn't really know him,* they would say, as if that excused their inconstancy. I couldn't do that. I loved with my entire body, with my whole black heart. I'd never stopped loving my father, even though he'd hurt me, even though he'd *stopped* hurting me. Even while he sat rotting in prison, hating me, I loved him like the innocent little girl I'd never really been.

I loved Hennessey. I feared Carlos. They twined together like thin strands of metal, a perverse braid, twisted and unbreakable.

I couldn't stop loving him even knowing what he was capable of. I could still turn him in. That was within my capability. But I'd hate myself for it. What else was new? The shower burned my skin, taking off chunks and swirling down the drain. The bruises on my body were no longer deep enough, wide enough for the indecision I felt inside.

After I dressed I headed to the Bureau for my meeting with Brody. That was the safest place for me anyway. The last thing I wanted was to be caught here by Carlos. Or worse, by one of his associates. He must know I suspected after leaving the hotel without saying goodbye. He must have known I'd figure it out, even if he had looked different. How had he done it? A disguise? It must be, but then I'd already known he was a master of them. I remembered the spread of grainy security camera shots with different clothes, different hairstyles.

He was a chameleon. Changing his hair color, his eye color had been child's play. His face structure had been different, the cheeks fuller and the forehead higher, but there were techniques people used to change those, fillers that went inside the mouth and cosmetic putty. These were things we learned at Quantico to help us detect disguises—and to help us go undercover.

Carlos.

I shook my head, not believing. Maybe I was imagining things. *God, please let me be imagining things.* I wouldn't mind going crazy if it meant I didn't have to face this choice again. This betrayal. Except I wasn't the one being betrayed. I was the one doing it, and that hurt so much worse.

I trust you, Hennessey had said last night. And he did, so much it tore me up inside. He didn't have to show me that side of him. He could have dated me as himself, had sex with me as himself. He even could have whipped me as himself, if he'd just told me he was into that BDSM shit. I would've done it.

But he'd wanted to show me the real side of him, the dark side. Just like I'd done for him last night. Something far more intimate than sexual intercourse. We'd told each other the truth. Oh, it had been tentative and framed with doubt, but we'd done it. We'd each offered up ourselves, our *true* selves, and he'd accepted me completely. He trusted me, and in repayment, I was going to walk into the Bureau and turn him in to my boss.

People would call me strong and smart. I might even get a commendation out of it. A promotion, a raise. So fucking brave they'd have to reward me. But I'd know the truth. It took more strength to stand beside someone you loved, even when they were wrong.

Especially when they were wrong.

The building bustled with its own nervous energy, expanding and shrinking like the bellow of a rough breath. The building heaved with inanimate panic. I crossed the marble floor with its scales of justice, feeling a sense of unreality. Of disbelief. They said justice was blind. They were right.

I nodded at a few agents I knew, gritting my teeth against the urge to scream. To cry. To ask for help. How many of them were on some drug lord's payroll? I bit the inside of my cheek to keep from screaming.

Laguardia had done more than hire an inside guy. He'd *been* the inside guy.

He'd made a fool of all of us. Me. Lance. Brody.

God. Brody. Would I tell him? I had to tell him. For anyone else, that was the easy answer. But I'd already sold out someone I cared about, and it hadn't worked out so well. Not for him and not for me. I wouldn't be tossed into the foster care system like garbage this time around. Wouldn't lose my childhood to overworked social workers and rats running in the space between the walls. No, this time around, I'd probably lose my life. With Carlos's wide-flung network and cold-blooded reputation, I would pay for this betrayal with my life.

"Coward," I muttered under my breath.

The irony was Brody might not even believe me, but I had to try. I owed that to the Bureau, didn't I? If not that, then I owed it to the men and women who might be hurt if I said nothing. People Carlos might hurt.

I headed straight for Brody's office, on a mission. Praying I could do this. Needing to stay silent. It was like flipping a coin into the air and finding out which side you wanted it to land on. Heads, and you finally, *finally* found someone in the world who understood you. Who accepted you. Tails, and you were responsible for his execution. Fuck.

"Sam?"

I didn't have time for Lance. I waved, trying to put him off. He refused.

"I need to talk to you," he said urgently.

"I have a meeting with Brody." My voice sounded unnatural. Flat. Was this really me?

Dissociation. Another fancy term the textbooks were fond of using. But one thing I'd figured out about labels early on: naming something didn't actually help you fix it. That was really all psychology was. It catalogued mental diseases, made neat little charts with symptoms and checkboxes. It couldn't cure a damn thing—least of all me.

Lance touched my elbow. "Please. It's about Hennessey."

That got my attention. "What about him?"

He cocked his head toward a corner, and I followed

him there, feeling numb and unafraid. The worst thing had already happened. Nothing else could faze me. At least, that was what I thought until he spoke.

"Hennessey is in trouble."

I narrowed my eyes. "What kind of trouble?"

Lance wouldn't meet my eyes.

"Shit. What did you do?"

He flushed. "I started digging, that's all. I wanted to know more about him. Make sure everything was on the up-and-up."

Oh God. Everything *wasn't* on the up-and-up. Had Lance figured that out as well? That would save me from having to tell Brody. But I found, inexplicably, that the idea of Hennessey being caught horrified me. Carlos was one thing, an abstract evil who'd done everything in his power to maintain that image. But Hennessey was a real person. A man. And I loved him.

How was it possible? I didn't know. How was it possible to kill and rape and steal and do a thousand other illegal things that Carlos had done? I didn't have the answer to that either, but despite all that, *because* of all that, the biggest travesty still seemed to be loving a madman.

Lance was going on about the timetables lining up, and I cringed, knowing what was coming.

"So look. I'm really sorry, but there's some pretty strong evidence that he's been in Carlos's pocket the whole time. Helping him evade arrest. Maybe even helping him kidnap you."

He didn't know. He thought Hennessey was just *helping* Carlos, which was pretty reasonable if he found some evidence linking them. He wouldn't know they were the same man, though. We didn't have enough surveillance to be sure of that. There were only grainy pictures that might or might not be him. Most of the people who had done business with him and seen him in person were dead now.

Except Mia.

No wonder he hadn't wanted to go question her. It wasn't because she wouldn't have anything useful to say. It was because she'd know. She would recognize him.

"What evidence?" I asked Lance, stalling for time. Would I tell Brody what I knew? Combined with whatever Lance had already found, it would almost surely be enough for an arrest. And a search warrant, which might uncover the truth. Even as an accomplice, he was looking at serious jail time.

"Hennessey tipped him off about the raid. Both times, probably. But the second one we know for sure."

"How?" Panic began a steady thrum in my chest.

He glanced toward the hallway and Brody's office, but it was empty. His eyes filled with anxiety. "I'm not even supposed to be telling you this, but he's going to be in that meeting with you and Brody. That's when it's going to come out. They're going to pull guys in, in case he tries to flee. But it might get dicey. I didn't want you walking in blind."

Oh Jesus. "I appreciate you cluing me in, but you're

accusing *my partner* of flipping on us. On me. I need to hear exactly what proof you have, and I need to know it now."

"Brody had me pull the cell tower records for the call you made while you were…"

"Kidnapped," I said flatly.

"Right. The phone was a throwaway, of course, but we wanted to see if anyone else had called that number, maybe get lucky with a lead. There was only one number that had called. Repeatedly. Another throwaway, but when we called it last night…" *Oh God.* I remembered hearing the phone ring. I remembered him ignoring it. "We were able to locate the cell tower it was closest to. The one right next to Hennessey's hotel. I had the address because I'd looked it up for you." He cringed, looking guilty. "I showed it to Brody this morning. He basically shit himself, and he's been on the rampage ever since. It's going to be bad."

Bad didn't begin to cover it.

"It could be someone else," I said lamely, but what were the odds that some other accomplice of Carlos was living in the same hotel? None at all. Besides, they would search him and find the phone. Further investigation might crack open the truth, that he *was* Carlos instead of just a man helping him.

Why was I so terrified? This solved my dilemma. Now Hennessey could go to jail, or worse, and I wouldn't have a hand in it. Not really.

Except that I had led Lance to him. Despite his dislike of the man, Lance never would have looked up where Hennessey was staying if I hadn't asked him to. When he'd seen the area pull up in the cell records—Montrose, not an area normally known for organized crime—he'd made the connection. Fuck. I'd already committed my betrayal last night, and I hadn't even known the truth at the time. My pulse beat heavily, marking an uneven pattern. I didn't want them to nail Hennessey. But it was out of my hands now.

The world rippled around me, underwater and surreal. Ignoring Lance's questions, I walked to Brody's office for my meeting. It didn't feel real. I wished it weren't. The beige hallway and the tightly woven carpet. The cluttered desk, as if this were just another day in the life of Special Agent Brody. As if he wasn't about to make the arrest of his career. He was the one who'd get a commendation now. A promotion, a raise. He greeted me with grave eyes that hinted at concern.

"Samantha," he said, more warmly than I'd ever heard him. "Are you sure you're up for this?"

As if you care, I wanted to yell. He was throwing me into the middle of a gunfight just so he could make his arrest, but he was concerned for me. What bullshit. "I'll be okay," I said.

He smiled. "Good. Just a little bit longer. Then it will all be over."

Asshole.

I sat down in the corner, my body still while my mind raced. What the hell was I going to do? Like staring at a train speeding toward me with only enough time to save myself. And leave the person I loved standing in the tracks. Could I do it? I had to.

If things did go badly, it would get violent. I wasn't carrying. My weapon hadn't been returned to me since my kidnapping. That was part of what would happen at the meeting today. But I realized now that would never have happened. Even without this impending arrest, he'd been planning to dismiss me. Honorably, of course. No doubt the staff psychologist would find a way to spin it for him. PTSD or some other bullshit. As if anyone could see the things we saw, could do the things we were paid to do and not get fucked up.

Anyway, I couldn't imagine Hennessey going quietly. He might protest the accusations, but if the evidence were compelling enough...if he knew he might get caught, his true identity exposed...he'd fight to get out.

Of course he would.

It would be self-defense.

I could rationalize anything, even a shoot up of my workplace. Unconditional love. But at least I wasn't lying anymore. Silently, hopelessly, I told myself the truth. I loved both sides of him, the fierce man and the broken monster.

Hennessey knew something was wrong the second he entered the room. He hadn't been expecting me in this meeting with Brody. He'd thought we'd be meeting separately, I could tell by the surprise he masked quickly, but that wasn't the real problem. Instead, he felt the tension in the air, scented it like an animal. I could see the options running through his brain as he took in Brody's expression and mine. Could see him lean toward the door and calculate his odds of making it out of an FBI office alive. Not likely. If he ran, they'd know he was guilty. That wasn't an FBI directive; it was just animal instinct. Run and the predators would come after you, mindless in their violence.

He sat down, greeting us both. "Brody. Holmes."

I nodded, my throat too dry to speak. *Run,* I wanted to shout, but that would be the worst betrayal of all. I looked at the closed door and tried to imagine how many guards Brody would have stationed there. With orders to stop anyone fleeing.

We were dead. So dead. Except…when had I started including myself in this ill-fated escape plan? Was I seriously going to run with him, to align myself with a criminal? I remembered telling him about the scorpion and the frog. He was right when he said I wasn't the scorpion. He was. As long as I stayed near him, he might hurt me. If the water didn't drown us first.

Brody cleared his throat and picked up a file, pretending to read it. "I'm glad you're both here. I've received some disturbing information, and I'd like to get it cleared up as soon as possible." He looked up at Hennessey. "I'd like to clear your name."

Hennessey raised his eyebrows, appearing both surprised and unafraid. It was a great act. He looked like an innocent man. "I wasn't aware it was dirty," Hennessey said lightly. "Mind filling me in with this information?"

If I hadn't already known the truth, I would have been outraged on his behalf. I'd have believed this lie.

"Last night, a phone call was placed to a disposable cell phone with known ties to Carlos." Brody studied him for a response.

He went unnaturally still. I could feel him remembering that moment in the hotel room, when the phone had rung. *Leave it.* Had he even checked it this morning? Or had he been too caught up in me? If I had distracted him, put him off guard, then this was my fault. Either way it was my fault, because only through my actions did they know where he'd been staying. It's not like agents were investigated on a daily basis. Only if something went wrong...or if the agent already knew the address and made the connection. Damn Lance and his competence. Damn myself for using him.

Hennessey remained stubbornly silent, waiting for the other man to state the accusation plainly.

Brody cleared his throat. "In fact...this is quite unfortunate...but we have information that you are staying in the same vicinity where that call went. Within a half-mile radius."

"I'm staying in a hotel." His voice was dry. "There are quite a few people living within a half-mile of me."

"That may be so, but the odds of them having ties to this case are low. You do. And the information you have, that you've had access to for some time. If you were to supply that to Carlos, it would be invaluable. I think we can all agree on that."

"That's hardly evidence of anything," Hennessey said, but I could feel him stalling, thinking. Looking for a way out, but there was none. I'd had a few minutes longer, and I'd already seen that. No escape.

"Not proof," Brody said, but it didn't feel like a concession. Instead, he leaned forward, a shark sensing blood in the water. "But if we find the phone on your person. Or in your hotel room. That's compelling. And if we dig a little farther…who knows what we'll find?"

If they dug deep enough, they'd find a criminal mastermind had been working under their noses all this time. Siphoning off information, misdirecting them. Maybe even using them against his competitors. It would be humiliating for the Bureau, and God, they would come down so hard. There'd be no coming back from that. Nothing but the death penalty would do.

So if I protected Hennessey, if I saved him somehow, it would be saving his life. I could justify anything. I used to tell myself lies. *No one has ever hurt me. You can be normal. Just pretend.* But Carlos had stripped away all that scar tissue, torn it off my body, leaving me bleeding and bared. Then Hennessey had put me back together, helped me heal. Two sides of the same man. And me in the middle.

"I brought the phone," I blurted out.

Both men looked at me with surprise.

"Carlos mailed it to me. I think he wanted me to call him." I tried to shrug. "I guess he thought he'd fucked with my mind enough where I'd be his informant."

"Carlos gave you the phone," Brody said flatly, his

disbelief clear.

And well he shouldn't believe me, since I was making it up. Lying for Carlos. Protecting Hennessey.

Deep breath. I had started this lie to save Hennessey. Now I had to follow it through. "Or maybe he just liked me. Maybe he wanted to fuck me again."

Neither man knew what to do with that. The poor abused girl, they were thinking. They were right—and wrong at the same time. No wonder they were confused. I was confused.

"So if you want to arrest me for that," I said. "Go ahead and do it. What do I care anymore?"

But they didn't arrest me. They couldn't, when I hadn't done anything wrong. Not really. I was the girl who'd been broken, the one being stalked by a maniac. And I'd taken the phone to my partner for help. There was no way they could authorize a search warrant or arrest. Not for me. And not for Hennessey. I'd protected him. And the way he stared at me, with surprise, with fierce intensity, he knew. He knew what I'd done and why I'd done it. He knew I'd kept him safe.

This was the end of the story as I knew it. I'd lived this once before. I knew the proper ending. The bad guy goes to jail, and the good girl lives alone, in fear. In shame. But I'd gone off script this time. I'd protected him instead.

What do you remember?

Nothing.

The past couldn't hold me any longer, and I had no idea what would happen next.

Chapter Sixteen

M Y STREET WAS dark, the heavy trees blocking most of the moonlight. The houses each had a different style, some Victorian, others a flat Californian layout. Mine was a miniature ranch house, sprawling on its little yard. The variation might have looked overwhelming or cheap, but each lawn was lush and green, each mailbox unique.

I knew every neighbor on the street, attended block parties, and waved to the kids at the bus stop in the mornings. It was a far cry from a cardboard-walled apartment in a shitty part of town, and that was exactly how I wanted it. It was a far cry, too, from the urban chaos of Montrose that surrounded Hennessey's little motel.

And even farther from the docks, the criminal underworld where Carlos had reigned.

For all I knew, he might be planning to kill me. Even though we'd skated past the FBI today, they might continue investigating. Even with Carlos presumed dead. So he'd be safer if I wasn't around to talk...unless he trusted me. And that would be the stupidest move of them all. I'd proven myself disloyal a long time ago.

A tricycle lay on its side on my sidewalk. Katy, the little girl from next door. Her house was dark now. She'd be tucked in bed, safe from the monsters who lurked outside. So what did that make me? The closing of my car door was loud in the stillness of the night.

I paused in the driveway, looking up. A royal blue sky peeked from between the shadowed pine boughs. No stars were visible. We were too close to the city for that. At least he wasn't in jail. At least, wherever he was, he could also see the sky.

The key jammed in the lock, and with a rough twist, I got the door open. Half the things didn't work in this old house, which I found charming. I'd always had an affinity for broken things.

My purse hit the wood flooring with a muffled thud. I kicked off my shoes beside it, but I didn't have the energy to put them away properly. I didn't have the energy to make dinner, either, but then my appetite had pretty well dried up. No, I had a singular goal, and that was my bed. I didn't even bother with the light. I was halfway through the living room when I froze. The only thing I heard was the low drone of the air conditioner. The only thing I saw were the vague dark shapes of my furniture. But somehow I knew I wasn't alone.

And the slightly warmer air told me who it was. Not unpleasant, really. Cozy. He didn't like it cold, and he'd changed my house to suit him.

"Hello, Samantha."

That voice. In the dark, tinged with a familiar accent,

it was Carlos.

"Hennessey," I said.

"You can call me Ian. I think we know each other well enough now that you can call me by my first name." The accent had disappeared. Like weaving in and out of shadows, he flashed light and dark.

"That's not really your name, though."

"Oh, but it is. You heard Brody go on about my reputation. I'm a distinguished agent with tenure."

"You were," I said, my voice trembling only slightly. "They aren't going to let you keep working there."

"No?" He sounded amused. "I think they will. I think Brody doesn't have any power that I don't give him. I'm personal friends with men two levels higher. I have a direct line to senators on the oversight committee. So no, I don't think Brody can do a fucking thing unless I approve of it."

The air felt impossibly thin, like we'd climbed to the top of a mountain. Standing on crumbling rock and surrounded by wispy clouds. And falling. If he'd been the one in charge all this time, then he was responsible for me being on the case. He'd even allowed *me* to remain his partner, when he could have refused me. And he let the bust go early.

Why? *To kidnap me.*

It felt strangely egotistical to even think of it. And yet, it was the solution that most made sense. He may not have known about me before he came to Houston, but once he met me, once he *wanted* me, he'd found a way to take me.

"Oh God," I whispered. "Oh Jesus." It was real. Until now, I couldn't be sure. I didn't want to be sure. I could come up with excuses for how he'd had that phone. Maybe he really *had* been an informant for Carlos, which would have somehow been better. At least his role would have been over, with Carlos dead. And I could have convinced him to fly straight from then on…

And now, too. He could be sitting in my house, after breaking and entering, because he wanted to surprise me. Like a date, while showing off his stealthy maneuvers and lock-picking skills. Even though I knew all of that was wishful thinking, and that this was the only answer, the true answer, I'd kept a small flame of hope alive.

"Are you going to fight me?" he asked, so idly he might have been asking about the weather. *Will it rain tonight?* he would wonder. And yes. God, yes. It would storm.

"Would it matter if I fought?"

"It would matter, yes. Would it stop me? No."

My muscles tensed for a flight not yet taken. Fear rooted me to the floor. Humiliation, hard and knotted in my stomach, kept me upright. Had he been *laughing* at me all that time? In the Bureau offices, and later, in the fucking warehouse? Knowing how scared I was. How helpless. *He made me helpless.*

"How dare you," I said, and my voice was shaking. Not with fear. With Rage. "You…you kidnapped me. You *hurt* me."

"You wanted it."

I had to laugh, harsh and metallic. It was too ridiculous. Too textbook. The excuse every asshole had ever given for hurting a woman. He'd hurt me. The awareness of it sank through me, wiping the brittle smile off my face. Not only then. Now. He hurt me now too.

"You don't really believe that." My voice was flat now. *Don't bullshit me*, it said.

"Oh, but I do. You want the darkness. I can give you that. So don't pretend with me. If you need to fight me, fine. If you need to cry, even better. But don't pretend like I'm not exactly what you've been looking for."

"Right," I said sarcastically. "You're the man of my dreams. Because you know me so well."

"What did you think my business was about? What did you think I traded in—drugs? Weapons?" He laughed, low and cruel. "Flesh?" There was a pause while my mind shouted *yes, that, exactly*. "No. I trade information."

He let that sink in before he continued.

"I knew everything about you before I ever laid eyes on you in that conference room. I knew you liked to eat scrambled eggs for breakfast and what your favorite antique store was. I knew about the foster brother who used to lock you in the closet. He paid for that by the way."

My eyes widened. Did he mean that he had—?

"And I knew about your father. I knew that you had lived in darkness, but it was only when I met you that I realized you craved it too. I told Brody not to put you on the team. I warned you away too. But there you were anyway, offered up on a platter."

"Why didn't you come to me?" I asked, half shouting, half pleading. "If you just wanted to be with me, why not just take me normally—"

"Normal?" he scoffed. "You wouldn't like me half as much if I were normal. I saw you, I wanted you, I took you. You want me to fucking apologize for that? No. This is how it works. I'm an animal, remember? A monster. You put a slab of fresh meat in front of me, this is what happens."

"Is that all I am to you?" I whispered. "A piece of flesh? Of meat?"

"*Yes*," he said, and the conviction in his voice didn't allow it to be an insult. "You're meat when I've been fucking starving my whole life, so fucking accept it. You're mine. *Mine*. Got it?"

I cried then, with fat teardrops down my cheeks. I cried because he was right about me, and how much I wanted him. And because he was wrong about himself. He wasn't an animal. He was the most intelligent, complicated person I'd ever met. He may not be good or virtuous, but he was human, flawed and powerful.

And I cried because he needed me too. I was the only one who could see past all the shit he had done, all the shit that had been done to him. Even Mia, as sweet and selfless as she was, only looked at him and saw a man to obey. I saw a man to worship, and that terrified me more than anything he could have done to my body.

I bolted. My heart pounding a staccato beat, I ran for the front door. I made it onto the porch before he slammed into me from behind. We flew into the air. He turned on his side, catching most of our weight on his shoulder and grunting on impact. I rolled to get up, but he already had a firm grasp around my waist and all I succeeded in doing was rubbing my body against his. It was clear almost immediately, from the tension in his body and the hard length against my thigh, that he was toying with me. A cat releasing his prey only to catch her again.

"Let me go," I gasped. "I'll scream."

"Do it." He was out of breath too, though I suspected for different reasons. Or maybe they were the same, after all. If I were honest, I could admit I wasn't fighting very hard. I wanted to *hurt* him. I just didn't want to get away.

"Asshole," I hissed.

He laughed unsteadily. "Rookie."

I moved to knee his groin—already erect, it would have really hurt—but he blocked me in time and pinned me to the porch. "Ah ah, be careful with that. If you break your toys, you don't get to play with them."

That was the problem, wasn't it? I liked my toys better broken.

It made me mad how much he knew me. He'd gotten under my skin before I'd even realized who he was. Then I did try to kick him, *hard*, but he already had the upper hand. All I succeeded in doing was flailing against the wooden boards and panting beneath him.

"So angry. What a pretty sight." He ran his thumb over my lips, which were pouting, I admit. It was childish, and I just barely held back from biting him. He would enjoy that too much. I glared up at him, mutinous, trembling inside.

His lids lowered. "Are you going to be good for me?"

"Never," I said, but with my lips parted around the word, he slipped his thumb inside. The invasion felt strange and complete, like something I should fight, like something I couldn't hope to fend off. I tasted salt and a sort of metallic flatness, like earth. My tongue tried to push him out, and only caressed him instead, licked him. His lower body surged against mine, reacting to the touch of my tongue. It was heady, that power, finally something I could control beyond kicking and screaming. Beyond throwing a temper tantrum. No longer child-like. A woman.

I closed my lips around his thumb and sucked, swirling my tongue around the tip and across the pad.

He groaned. "Your mouth feels so good. I can't wait to fill it with my cock."

My breath caught. "Dirty talk?" I managed. "That's new."

"Yes, well, I'm full of surprises."

I laughed, breathless. That was the understatement of the year.

He sat back and pulled me up. "Let's go inside. I

didn't make it this far to get arrested for public indecency."

There it was again, a sly omission to his true identity. I wondered if he'd ever spell it out for me, if he could trust someone that much. A conversation could be recorded or at least recounted for a court of law. This innuendo, not so much.

It felt surreal to know that one of the FBI's Most Wanted was in my house. I tried to tell myself this was serious, that it was bad. But if he wanted to hurt me, he could have already done it. He might still do it. There wasn't much I could do to stop it from happening, if it was going to, so there was no use worrying about it.

That might have been a strange reaction. Maybe normal people were supposed to get scared when their abuser stalked and attacked them. But this was me, with my past, and I could only feel relief. Like falling off a cliff and laughing on the way down. Crazy from the perspective of those solid and safe on the ground. But in the air, with the wind in my face, the sheer momentousness transformed loneliness into respite, fear into joy.

He led me to my bedroom, walking in front of me instead of carrying me—both tender and commanding all at once. Then I had stirred only to find him gone. Here, now, I found the same thing. He hadn't followed me inside.

I looked back and realized Ian stood in the doorway.

"Invite me in."

"What, are you a vampire?"

He laughed darkly. "Why, afraid I'll take your blood?"

The words sent a shiver down my spine. He'd drawn blood when he'd taken me. But he'd stopped shortly after that. He'd hurt me, and he'd been careful with me. He'd kidnapped me and cared for me. Our moments together were strung together with extremes, skating the edges before coming to rest in the middle.

"Come here," I asked softly.

And he did, taking me in his arms and pushing me back on the bed. We fell together, landing in a sensual tangle of limbs and light. The windows had old lacy coverings that hung open. Neither of us made a move to push them closed. Neither of us turned on the light. I wanted to see him just like this, in silvery shadows. Without the fluorescent office lighting, without the blindfold. His body was made of reflection like this, the line of his hip and the curve of his bicep. Sleek muscles over bone, coarse skin sprinkled with hair. A beautiful male body that curved around me and pressed against me.

He touched and moved and conquered me until I gasped, breathless and naked. Modesty and shame meant nothing with him. There was a rare form of security with a man who had broken laws just to be with me, a surety that he wanted my body, craved it beyond normal reasoning.

And he proved it again in the way that he caressed me, not with hands and mouth. That would be too ordinary for him. With a pinch and drawn breath. Squeezing to the point of pain and a tear that fell from the corner of my eye. With a desperate shuddering sigh that made me run a finger along his brow. So much pain inside that he had to cause it to find relief. And that was fine. I was strong enough to take it. My body writhed, and my stifled cries filled the room, but I never told him to stop. Never wanted him to.

He licked my nipples, slow and tender. Then bit me, so hard it felt like I would bleed. I didn't bleed though, not on the outside. Only inside, where it felt like I'd never come together again. Where bleeding wasn't death, it was release. Where all my hopes and fears could spill into the air around us, leaving me pure and unbroken.

His mouth moved over my whole body, writing on me, marking me, and I gasped and writhed at the pleasure and pain sensations. He didn't pause at my breasts. Didn't stop at my sex.

He skated over the slippery lips of my cunt and kept going. The curve of my hip was just as interesting to him, the soft inner flesh of my thigh. The hollow of my ankles caught his attention and held it. Every square inch of my skin held fascination for him, and he stayed to suckle and soothe until I was rocking my hips into the air and begging, begging.

"Please, more. Come inside me. *Please.*"

His laugh was pure masculine conceit. "Where? Here?"

A sudden thrust and two fingers were inside me,

stretching me. I gasped at the intrusion and clenched down hard, wanting more. More sweet pain and more aching fullness.

"But who do you want here, hmm?"

Carlos, he meant, or Hennessey? I panted. "You. Only you."

"How do you know? What if I hurt you?" He twisted his fingers, finding a spot inside me and ruthlessly pressing it.

I groaned at the feeling. *So close.* But not enough to come. "The only way you could hurt me is to leave."

He froze for a second. I thought he might really leave then, and it was on the tip of my tongue to call him back.

A surge of emotion blazed in his eyes, lighting up the dark. His eyes fell shut, but they didn't shut me out. They drew me deeper, into knowing him, into feeling every wish he'd ever had. For money, for power. All means for the same damn thing. So that no one could control him. So that no one could ever get close enough to make him care. So that no one could ever shoot the only person he cared about while he stood by, small and helpless.

But he did care about me, and in a twisted way, I held this control over him. He wouldn't leave. I saw the answer in his eyes: he couldn't. He pressed his fingers deeper and placed rough biting open-mouthed kisses on my belly, my thighs. He devoured me, and I cried my gratitude into the night.

It felt like being with him for the first time. Not the monster who bound and whipped me. Not the tender lover who let me take the lead. Both of those were facets of him, light shining onto a certain part of him. This was the rock at the center, the one without fear or artifice.

I had exposed him, found out his secrets, threatened his life with the knowledge I held, and instead of retaliation, he'd come here to...what? To fuck me. To make love to me. They both sounded wrong for the unadulterated need infusing his every touch. I didn't have a vocabulary for what he did to me, but then no one had been able to define the man himself. An enigma, an abomination, a wish on a star. He consumed me, and I drifted inside him, blissed out on the ride.

I didn't know how he would dominate me, but I knew that he would. It was in his genetic make-up. His past may have sharpened the edges, made walls where there had been none, but he would always be a man who took control.

I had been tested too young, abused and discarded before I even understood the dynamics of sex. But I always would have been a loyal creature, one who would guard my territory with no holds barred, a woman who prized strength and survival above all else.

He moved beside me, still licking and biting down my body. Down to my cunt, but instead of kneeling between my legs, he straddled me facing down. The sixty-nine position, but with him on top, and though he didn't put all his weight on me, I could still feel his warm, hard presence above me. My arms were pinned at my side by his legs around my shoulders. My head was caught inches from where his cock hung heavy and thick. He spread my legs below, pressing me against the sheets.

His lips felt like bliss against my cunt. He tongued me from my clit down to the bottom, and I rolled my hips up into his mouth. It was a form of bondage, being unable to move, unable to see. But I was bound only by his body, surrounded only by him, and I breathed in deep to cherish it. He lapped at my sex, without insisting I do anything for him, but I knew. I knew what I was supposed to do, what I longed to do, and I lowered my head to take his cock into my mouth. The tip was slick and salty with his pre-come, and I licked it off, swallowing it down. Then there was nothing but the smooth head of his cock, the thin slit and the ridged underside. I explored him with my tongue, memorizing every curve and hollow, imprinting every jagged moan onto my mind. What he liked and how he liked it. I wasn't sure if we would ever be together after this, so I furrowed out each bit of knowledge, savored each sensitive place as if this were our last chance.

He began to move his hips, thrusting his cock inside my mouth. I held my head steady, letting him fuck my head that way while I tried to caress him with my tongue. He fucked me down below as well, with his tongue, while his fingers walked down the taut skin and circled my asshole. I clenched there, nervous and willing.

He pressed one finger against the puckered opening

and slid only barely inside. It still felt like too much, too full, enveloped now by his body, swallowing his cock, fucked by his tongue, and invaded at that one forbidden point. Too much, and I bucked against him, making everything worse until it became suddenly better, bursting into a thousand sun-bright rays and drifting back to the shadows that had made me.

He turned, moving over me with stealth and a quickness born of necessity. His body was beautiful in the moonlight, made of some foreign substance, silver and bright. His cock reentered me with his knees on either side of my head, with him facing me.

He looked down at me as he fed me his cock, muttering, "Take it. Fast now. That's right, good. *Yes.*"

I opened my mouth and accepted every hot pulsing inch. He was close. I could see it in the jerkiness of his movements and the flare of his nostrils. He was an animal facing death, fight or flight, and for his choice he pressed his hips against my face, rubbing the crinkly hair at the base against my nose. I swallowed around him. It hurt, but I barely noticed in my haze. The world went dim with the loss of breath. Black spots in front of my eyes. Then his cock flexed once, twice, and something liquid and warm slid down my throat. As he pulled back to let me breathe, the last drops of his come trailed over my tongue, sharp and sweet.

The taste of him lingered long after the liquid was gone. His expression was dark and severe, unreadable in the shadows. He didn't tell me I pleased him, but I knew anyway. I knew from the way he didn't correct me, and he would have. I knew from the tender way he pulled me into his arms.

Whips and chains seemed suddenly superfluous, so much wrapping around a gift already given. His command and my obedience, both implicit in our actions, too firmly rooted to need words. He didn't need to bolt me down when I would stay by his side. And if I wouldn't, if I flitted away, if I betrayed him after all…well, then I had never really been his.

CHAPTER SEVENTEEN

H E WAS FLIPPING through a stack of CDs when I came back into the room. He lifted one. "Do you mind?"

"Why would I?"

He'd already beaten and kidnapped me. His sardonic expression said he understood the subtext of my shrug. Well, fuck him and his smugness. I wanted him to come back to bed. We had slept for a few blissful hours and then had woken to make love again. A clinging, bruising love that might have scared someone else. Instead, I found the answers to questions I'd had my whole life. Since I'd let my foster brother "get lucky" with me at age fifteen, and then a senior at school the next year, I'd known something was missing. *This.*

I had lied to myself, pretending I could be normal, pretending I even wanted to be normal. But why would I want to be someone different than I was? Did normal people secretly yearn to be deviant? I didn't know, but I could no longer pretend. No longer hide when a man who felt the same way stood in my bedroom.

With the press of a button, the sweet strains of "The Music of the Night" drifted from the stereo speakers.

Something hollow inside me began to fill, an emotion, an understanding.

When I'd first met Hennessey in that conference room, I'd thought he was like Police Inspector Javert, on a lifelong quest to uphold the law at any cost. That would mean that Carlos was Valjean, the criminal, the hunted. Two separate men.

And then later, after I'd met Mia, I'd thought he was like Dr. Jekyll, the well-intentioned doctor with questionable means. And his other face, Mr. Hyde. A monster. Two sides of the same man.

But now, the man who had found me in the shadows, who had dragged me to bed and wrapped his body around mine...now I knew he was the *Phantom of the Opera*. Always hiding, always wanting.

One man. All along he'd been one man, and I could see all of him now, whole and unbearably human.

I shivered, and he must have felt it, because he pulled a blanket up to my chin. It wasn't cold out, though. It was a warm Houston summer and the A/C in this old house could barely keep up. His body burned like a furnace, but I wouldn't have moved for anything. I didn't want the cold reality to intrude on the peace we'd found. So fragile, that peace. Like the human body. Like hope. He didn't like the cold because he longed for a connection as much as I did. We were too different to find that at some corporate holiday party or an awkward first date. But we found it here, with each other.

"What happened to your partner?" I asked into the

dark.

There was a pause. "He got too close. Started asking questions, so many questions. I told him to back off. I *told* him."

"Did you kill him?"

His body turned rigid. "Fuck. Is that what you thought?"

Yes. "Maybe."

"I didn't kill him." His laugh was bitter. "I warned him, though. Told him what would happen. He didn't listen. He went to visit one of my...one of Carlos's associates. Not a nice man. They had a chat. Then when my partner turned to leave, he was shot in the back."

I swallowed hard in the silence.

"All for doing the right thing." He sounded incredulous. "All for doing his job. I killed the man who murdered him. He was sorry, in the end, but it's not enough."

No, it wasn't enough. Strange that he could see that, a man who had been born to a life of violence. But then, he'd become an FBI agent.

"Did you always plan it this way?" I asked softly. Had he always planned to betray the FBI? Which came first, the chicken or the egg?

He knew what I meant. "I was born to the king of a drug cartel. In those days, they really were like royalty, especially in Colombia where they lived. My mother was the daughter of some mafioso in New York, who sold her to solidify their business partnership. She was fourteen at the time."

My heart hurt to think of a young girl—a child, really—being forced to marry a grown man. Forced to move to a different continent, where she may not have even spoken the language. But most of all, my heart hurt because of the quiet way Ian spoke of his mother.

"My father was the worst kind of asshole. He beat her, of course. The memories I have of her, we're hiding. In the closet or under some piece of furniture. It wasn't when he was drunk or angry. It was all the time. And she would sing to me. Quietly, under her breath. She never stopped, even though I realize now she must have been tired, her throat would have been sore. But her only thought was for me."

I swallowed thickly. I knew how the story ended—with his mother's brutally quick murder. But I hadn't been able to comprehend then how much her death would have cut him. Slayed him.

The need to confess tickled my lips. He had a right to know. "Mia told me," I admitted. "How she died. How you came to run the cartel."

He stiffened, his body rigid behind me. For a second I was sure he would leave. Then he sighed. "Mia. Well, my father always said that women were a weakness. And for me, he's been right. Twice."

I shivered a little with the knowledge that he was talking about me.

"You loved her," I said. Not a question. A statement of fact. Only if he loved her would he have confided in her that way. The way he was doing with me now.

"I still love her. I always will, but she's better off where she is now."

Yes, that was undeniably true. A loving, protective husband and a white house with a flowerbed. It was an idyllic life…and one that Ian had given to her, as a gift. He would have mourned that loss. He would have missed her.

"You gave her up," I said softly.

"Yes."

I had to turn then. In his arms, facing him. The shadows illuminated the curve of his cheek, the silver hair at his temples. He was made of shadows and reflected light, unreal even while I felt him solid and warm in front of me.

"And me?" I asked. "Will you give me up too? Keep me for a while, use me? Then turn me over when I fall in love with some wholesome FBI agent?"

"No," he snarled the word. "That won't happen. I wouldn't let it."

I stared at him, shocked by his vehemence but still disbelieving.

His voice softened. "The way I feel about you is different."

My heart thudded a warning. "You don't love me?"

"Not like that. I wanted to break her. I did everything I could to break her, but it never worked. I'd always stop at the last minute, pull back before delivering the final blow. Or maybe she was stronger than any of us realized. Either way, it didn't happen. I couldn't break her, so I had to give her away."

"You wanted to break her, but not me." My lips twisted in acknowledgement. "I'm already broken."

He kissed my forehead. "You're the strongest person I've ever met."

A shift happened inside me, a newfound certainty. He saw me. He *knew* me. And he still wanted me, just as I was. It had seemed like an impossible dream at one point in my life, though I couldn't stop searching, even then. Who could love a monster? I was the monster, and he loved me.

His hand slipped down my neck and cupped my breast. He plumped the weight in his roughened palm. He pinched my nipple between his thumb and forefinger. Lightly at first, then harder. Pain shot through my body, and I yelped.

"You didn't think I was going to go easy on you, did you?"

I shook my head where it rested against his arm. That was one of the things he loved about me, my resilience. And one of the things I loved about him—his ferocity. The way he took what he wanted, and he wanted me.

Turning me, he straddled my waist, pinning me to the bed. He played with my breasts with both hands, molding and pinching while I writhed beneath him.

"I want to fuck you so hard I'd bruise you. I want to make you bleed."

"Are you always such a romantic?" I retorted.

"No." He squeezed my flesh until I cried out. Then he caressed it. "Would you rather I fuck a hundred other women the way I'm supposed to? Or would you rather I fuck one the way I want to?"

I gritted my teeth against the pain. "The choice isn't mine."

"You're right. It's mine. And I chose you."

He twisted me harshly, and I sobbed out a wordless protest. It lessened the blow of his words, though I still felt them ringing through me. *And I chose you.* I had been wrong before. It *was* romantic, what he said, what he did. Even while he hurt me, I had his full focus, his complete attention. His care, like worship. His love, an obsession. He slapped my breast and watched the force of his blow shape me. My full breasts always returned to their rounded shape, only reddened after the abuse. He slapped them again and again, until low moans escaped me. Tears streamed down the sides of my face. Mindless, my hands reached up to push him away. I didn't mean to make him stop, but the body will naturally protect itself.

It didn't matter. He pinned my wrists above my head and continued his torture. He was hard again, his cock thick and throbbing on my belly. I stared down at him, enthralled by the reddened skin and glistening tip.

He slapped my face. Softer than he'd done to my breasts but still a shock. I met his gaze.

"Sadist," he said with a slight smile.

"Liar," I accused breathlessly.

"Sociopath?"

"Better."

Still keeping my wrists bound, he bent his head and kissed my breasts. He licked them, soothing the hot, abraded skin. He dropped kisses along the upper slope of my breast, up the gentle dip at my throat and to my ear. He nibbled there and bit down gently.

"I don't need your consent," he murmured.

My swallow felt thick. "You have it."

"I know."

Reaching down, he pried my legs apart. Instinctively, my legs pressed together. With my wrists held together above me, and my body tense, I was too vulnerable, too scared. That didn't matter either. He opened me up as if I were nothing, a newspaper he split apart and shook to straighten. His cock slipped inside, the broad head parting my damp cunt. He didn't stop at the tip, didn't give me time to adjust. He pushed inside until his cock filled me completely, until he bottomed out. He released my thighs then, but not to let me go.

He placed his hands around my neck. And squeezed.

I breathed deep and frantic, trying to keep it together. I knew my eyes were wide in shock and effort.

"Shhh." He rained kisses down my temple, in praise, in comfort.

His hands tightened and released, testing me. Hurting me. I choked against the barrier, gasping, struggling to breathe. He loosened only to clench around my neck, working toward his pleasure, finding it in my frantic breaths—drinking them down in a kiss.

He set up a slow but steady pace that I could barely keep track of. A low groan came out of his lips, spurring me. My hips bucked up to meet him. I tried not to fight his hold on my throat. I failed.

My whole body jerked within the confines of his. He kept me prisoner and used me brutally, and I had to try to escape, jerking and whimpering and clenching around his cock. He sped up the pace, and I could only hold my mouth open.

My vision was too blurry with tears, my ears too full of my own stilted breaths. I felt his release though, the sudden tightening of the bonds all over my body. His body covering mine and his hand on my neck. His cock deep inside me as it spilled its warm seed.

When he finally freed me, I gasped blindly for breath, safe and secure in his arms. With a pleased sigh, he lay down beside me and pulled me close. I tucked myself against his body, barely registering the subtle rocking motion of my hips. It turned me on, what he did to me. It wasn't even his actions, really. I could have been roughly fucked by a hundred guys and never felt like this. Like he'd been desperate for me. Like he'd taken me.

"From now on, you wait for my permission to come. And you're only going to get it with my body. Understand?"

"Yes. *Please.*"

With a slight smirk, he nudged me over him so that I

was straddling his leg. A blunt push at my hips showed me what to do. My body felt strung up tight, sharp need constricting my cunt. Lowering myself, I pressed the slick skin against his thigh and rocked hesitantly. The coarse smattering of hair on his skin created extra friction against the lips of my sex, against my clit. I rocked faster, more sure now, finding my rhythm. The humiliation of the position roared through me, making me hotter. I closed my eyes, savoring the faint flavor of him still on my tongue from before. It wasn't enough, though. I draped my body against his, rubbing more than my pussy, rubbing my whole body, my breasts against him until the pleasure built and crested, and I came in hard, painful pulses, spilling liquid arousal all over his skin. I kept rubbing him until the last of the aftershocks had subsided.

Lazily, my eyes opened. Self-consciousness suddenly assailed me as I realized he'd been watching me this whole time. He'd seen my body in orgasm; he'd seen my face in rapture. All with his hands resting behind his head, as if he were watching a show. But his expression disarmed me. It was intent, focused. Reverent.

"Beautiful," he said.

Blushing, I lay down beside him again, curling myself into him. On the outside, it hadn't looked so different than regular sex. On the inside, though, the ground had shifted right under me. Sex was no longer a thing I did to be normal. It wasn't a favor I did for a horny guy at a bar. It was an experience shared. A connection found.

CHAPTER EIGHTEEN

I WOKE UP the next morning with a warm, empty space on the sheets beside me. The running water from the bathroom clued me in to Ian's location. As did the baritone voice singing off key. It made me smile, that off note. A reminder that he was human too, after all.

Until I registered the sad, lilting strains of *La Bohème*.

My smile faded. If I'd needed any further proof that this was the man who had held me captive, I had it. Not that there had been any question after his admissions. Or the way he fucked me. That I could have recognized blindfolded—and had been blindfolded.

I pushed myself out of bed and slipped into my running clothes. Every day at 6:00 a.m. I'd gone running since high school when I'd had ripped hand-me-down tennis shoes. The only time of day when the dingy streets were free and clear of the dealers and crack heads. At Quantico, where the miles I ran alone were piled on top of the strict fitness regimen in the academy. And in my own home, with sleek running clothes and ergonomic shoes that had come out of my first paycheck.

A running path drew curlicues around a manmade

lake a mile away from my house. I jogged a foot away from the curb until I reached it, then continued on the gravel path. I lost myself in the activity—my body and mind absorbed in the task. So I almost didn't notice him lounging near the bridge. He leaned against the base of the bridge, like a troll I had to answer to before I could pass. I slowed then stopped before joining him on the dewy grass.

"Nice morning," he commented.

I didn't have the patience for small talk. "Why are you here?"

His eyebrow rose, but he didn't reprimand me. Maybe he would walk on eggshells after what had happened to me. Or maybe what he was about to say was that bad.

"I figured you'd want to know the results of the psych eval."

Shit. *Focus.* I ran a hand over my face. Already there was a light sheen of sweat from my exertions. "I take it the results aren't good, since you felt the need to tell me in private."

"No, not bad. We just didn't get a chance to discuss in the meeting…after the incident with…" Agent Brody coughed. "The psychologist was generous. Six weeks' rest and you can get re-checked. Standard procedure, considering."

Considering I'd been tortured and sodomized, yeah. Not too bad. As expected. If he was expecting me to be grateful, though, he'd have to wait a long time.

A slight frown line appeared in his forehead. "I want

you to know that I'm looking out for you. I don't think a commendation is out of order for your dedication to service. A promotion, maybe a few months down the road."

"Really."

He must have mistaken that for enthusiasm, because he nodded quickly. "Yes, even though you broke protocol. You were doing it to assist your teammates, after all."

Ah, so that was how it would be. A cover-up to save all our asses. Having an agent captured by the target wouldn't sit well with the higher ups. Sure, I could get fired for my own part—the break in protocol—but Brody would be in hot water too. He was the one who'd pushed for the early run we weren't ready for. He was the one who'd assigned a junior officer to the case.

"Why did you put me on the case?"

He appeared surprised by my question, and maybe a little worried. "It wasn't my idea. I mean, I'd have you assist from the office, but not a principal. Not Hennessey's partner."

A force was welling up inside me, like a tidal wave, already cresting with frothy white foam. "Why then?"

Brody ran a hand over his face. He looked suddenly exhausted and a thousand years old. This job had taken its toll. Was that me in thirty years?

"The decision came from above my pay grade." His shoulders slumped. "They'll deny it now that it all went to hell."

"Why me? Because I looked like her, like Mia? Because I was his type?"

Confusion clouded Brody's expression. "Looked like who?" He shook his head. "Because of your past. We shouldn't have used that. If anything, we should have been mitigating the risk, not putting you directly in its path."

"I don't understand. What does my past have to do with…"

In truth, I knew the connections all too well. The invisible lines connecting the past to the present were deep and well-trodden grooves. But the FBI didn't know how much I struggled with my past. And they really didn't care.

"Because you would get the job done." Brody spoke as if it were obvious. "We've had problems with agents turning to the other side. Getting duped. They meet someone new, make a new friend…next thing we know they're moving to Alaska and switching professions. They're out of contact. They're susceptible. A weak point. Too many fucking weak points."

"And I'm not weak," I said, disbelieving.

"You're ambitious. That's what all your professors said. Driven. Fearless."

God. Those professors thought I was ambitious because I slept with them. Driven. Fearless. Only that hadn't been why at all. I aced those tests without their help, because I knew every word of every textbook. I'd slept with them because of my own brokenness, like tracing the fault lines over my body with their grasping hands.

"Top of your class," Brody continued. "You can outrun and outshoot every one of your male counterparts."

"So I'm...what? A secret weapon? A Trojan horse that no one would suspect of being deadly?" A living weapon, specially groomed by the FBI academy.

"Yes." He laughed, and the sound sent chills down my spine. "Exactly that. Heartless. You wouldn't be swayed by a bribe or intimidated by some crony of his."

I hadn't been bribed or intimidated by a crony of his; I'd been seduced by the man himself. I'd fallen in love with him.

Heartless.

They didn't know me at all. That was as good a reason to betray them as any. I let him stew for a few tense moments before putting him out of his misery. "Don't worry. I'll sign off on whatever story you put out."

He sighed in clear relief that the department's secrets would be safe.

In fact, he had no idea how safe. The good little girl had nodded her head. Anything for approval. I would bury this secret beside all the deeper, darker secrets that I'd guard with my life. Like the true identity of Ian Hennessey. Like the fact that Carlos was alive and well— and currently lounging in my house.

I was going to keep him from killing ever again.

Wasn't that enough? It was more than Brody could have done without my help. Maybe I had lived up to all that Trojan horse potential after all.

Brody was still talking. "Great, so in six weeks, you can call the office and make an appointment to come in for another psych eval. I'm sure you'll get an all clear at that point. Once you've been on the job for a few months, I'll be happy to reward you for your dedication and effort to the cause. I just can't make it too close together, you see. I can't have anyone wondering about your leave of absence and the promotion right after, you understand."

"Right." My voice was flat. "It would probably be a good idea if you didn't speak to me again. So that no one gets the wrong idea."

His face lit up. "Yes, exactly. It's a plan. Thank you, Samantha. I knew you'd understand."

I turned to leave. At the top of the bank, I looked back. "Oh, and Brody?"

He waited expectantly.

"I quit."

WHEN I GOT back to the house, the savory aroma of eggs and bacon greeted me. I paused in the doorway, unable to fully comprehend the sight of him cooking breakfast in my kitchen. Neither Carlos nor Hennessey was suited to this role. Lover. Companion. But this man, he was still an unknown quantity. It suited him to have a new name. I called him Ian, and for me, now, that was who he was.

"Are you going to come in?" He sounded amused.

Still wary, I went to the fridge and grabbed a cold water bottle. I sat at the old wood table, the same place I'd once searched through design schematics, looking for the man who sat beside me. That was how it had always been for me, searching desperately for the answer I already knew.

Ian slid a plate of steaming food in front of me, then set another place for himself.

"Orange juice?" he asked.

My life was surreal. "No thanks, but I'll take some coffee if there's any left."

He poured me a mug. "Milk?"

"Yes, please."

Though when I got my coffee, all I could do was stare at it. All I could do was stare at the beautiful meal in front of me and the beautiful table and wonder how the hell I'd gotten here.

"How was your run?"

I tilted my head, thinking of Brody. Thinking of quitting. "Refreshing."

"Good. Now tell me what's bothering you."

"Am I so obvious?"

"Not really. But I'm good at reading people."

Yes, he was. It was probably how he'd managed to pull this off, playing people off each other. Showing them what they wanted to see. And *that* was what bothered me now.

"How do I know this is real?"

"Why, does it seem like a dream? Maybe you're still tied up in my lair, floating through subspace and dreaming of coffee."

He had the most evil sense of humor. A smile played at my lips.

"How do I know *you* are real?" I asked, and this time he didn't make a joke. He understood what I meant. The FBI Agent or the Most Wanted picture. The light or the dark.

"I realize you may not believe me, but I have always been real around you. Except for what I did for my job, every word I ever spoke to you was the truth."

The same as it had been in captivity, I remembered.

He took a swallow of coffee as if fortifying himself. "The truth is, I spent most of my life not knowing who I was. I didn't want to be my father, but I knew I'd never fit in as a law enforcement officer either. Everything I did felt like a part to play, like I was going through life trying on different masks."

Like the stage. Maybe that was why the plays had always stuck with me, not only for their content. The prospect of living different lives, of being different people. But if these personas were only masks we wore, then we could discard them. We would be more vulnerable that way. Exposed. Free.

"Do you know who you are now?" I asked softly.

He leveled me with a look so intense and so open

that I felt the impact in my gut. "I know I don't want to be Carlos Laguardia anymore. I've been taking it apart, his legacy. It's not a quick or painless process. If I had walked away, the vultures would have snapped up the pieces. The only way to be sure it's really gone is to break it myself."

I remembered Brody telling me about the recent upheaval within the organization. *This is our best chance to bring them down*, he'd said. Except Hennessey was already doing it, from the inside. He'd done more than abdicate the throne; he was dismantling a criminal empire. It was the same thing he'd been tasked to do as an FBI agent, but the rigid laws and procedures could never have reached deep within the organization. Only he could do that.

"And Ian Hennessey?" I asked.

"Retiring. I've worked enough to get a little pension coming."

I raised an eyebrow. "Don't tell me you gave everything up? All of Carlos's money?"

He shrugged. "I've never been a fan of parties or mansions. Islands, though, those I can get behind. I always thought I'd end up living on one. Just get away from it all."

My nose scrunched in distaste. "I hope you're not planning on me joining you."

His eyes lit with amusement. "You aren't a fan of the beach?"

"The setting is fine. It's the seclusion that would

drive me crazy. I'm a little bit of a loner, but I still like to see people every once in a while."

"There are people on a private island. Someone has to sweep the seaweed off the sand."

I snorted. "I don't think the FBI pension covers buying an island."

"I have a few investments put away," he admitted. When I was quiet, he quirked a brow. "Anything else?"

So many questions. And not enough courage to hear the answers. However, there was one interesting fact about Ian Hennessey I already suspected…

Just thinking about it brought a sly smile to my lips. "And you have a foot fetish."

A slight flush tinged his cheeks and the tops of his ears. God, that was adorable. Someone this evil had no right to look adorable. He'd committed crimes against humanity, but he was shy about this.

"Perhaps," he said.

I almost rolled my eyes. "Perhaps? So when you beat the soles of my feet and then kissed them later, you were on the fence about it?"

The look he sent me was dire—and all warning. No follow through. The man had a thing for feet, for sure.

"Okay, so, it shouldn't really matter if I…" Beneath the table, I touched my toes to his ankle. And then slid upward, along his denim-clad shin. "If I do this. You don't care, right?"

A muscle ticked in his jaw. His eyes had gone intense and needful and practically fucking me with a glance.

"You're playing with fire, love."

Love. The endearment did strange things to my insides. I didn't stop though, didn't let up. I trailed my foot along the inside of his thigh, reveling in the way his muscles tensed and pulsed beneath my toes.

His lids lowered. He muttered a curse under his breath.

I smiled, feeling worldly and entirely sexual. I'd never found feet particularly sexy before, but this was something else. *He* found it sexy, and so I did too. The way he responded, as if I'd done the hottest thing possible, as if I'd blown his mind, made it so worth it.

Men had responded to blowjobs with less obvious enjoyment, closing their eyes and remaining stoic. Not Ian. I didn't have my mouth on his cock. We were both wearing all our clothes. But his cheeks were flushed, his eyes shadowed with arousal. He stared at me, begging, demanding. He muttered curse words in English and Spanish, like music to my ears.

I felt the ridge of his erection and wriggled my toes. His breath stuttered audibly, and his body jerked in the chair. God, he was beautiful. Held by the string of his arousal, helpless at my feet.

A knock came from the front door.

I jolted up, immediately nervous. My foot fell to the ground. What if Brody had decided to follow me home and convince me to come back? What if someone at the Bureau had decided to look into Ian after all?

Ian looked pissed at the interruption, but I felt his

alertness as well, a subtle flexing in his body. He looked like a man frustrated he wasn't getting sex, simple as that, but his concern bled through. This was how he managed to fool everyone. But I had gained intimate knowledge of his body, like truth-colored glasses that allowed me to see the real him.

Straightening, I brushed off my hands. I schooled my expression to calm.

At the door, Lance stood on the porch. The screen and its curlicue metal design obscured him, but I could see his fierce expression. He looked older somehow. And taller.

"Lance," I murmured, opening the screen door. "How are you?"

He nodded in greeting. His gaze inspected me, searching for something. Signs of abuse, maybe. Old bruises.

I drew his attention up, speaking gently. "Hey. What are you doing here? Shouldn't you be at the office?"

"I had to see you. Brody told us you weren't coming back."

Damn, that was fast. Not that I minded, exactly. It was a bit like ripping off a Band-Aid. Better to do it fast, even if it hurt. Like taking off a mask. Better to do it off-stage, so the audience never saw the real me.

"I'm sorry," I said. And I was. I'd liked working with Lance. But I loved Ian.

I felt his presence behind me. He rested his hand on the doorframe, sort of leaning over me, protective.

Possessive. Men—in every culture, they were the same. Whether law-abiding or criminal, the same. Like Martinez had done for Mia. I had to admit, I kind of loved it.

Lance didn't, though. His eyes darkened at the sight of Hennessey in my house. Hair rumpled. Wearing a white undershirt. Clearly he had stayed the night.

"Can I speak to you privately?" Lance asked me in a low voice.

"Sure."

With a warning look at Hennessey I stepped onto the porch. I may have found Hennessey's possessiveness endearing, but the last thing I wanted was a pissing contest. For one thing, there was always a chance it could lead to more questions about Ian. The farther we got away from the FBI, the better.

But I also felt guilty. I hadn't wronged Lance. If anything, he was the one who ratted me out to Brody. Still, I felt responsible for what had happened. For involving him. For existing.

Transitive guilt.

I sighed, accepting. "I'm sorry."

His gaze sharpened. "For what?"

"For not telling you first. You're my friend. You shouldn't have had to hear it from Brody."

"I don't give a shit about who I heard it from. I care that you're not coming back. Why? Are the...are your injuries not getting better?"

"That's not it. I'm healed." What a strange concept,

healed. If I'd ever been broken, it had been years ago. Ancient history, like some sort of Egyptian myth. Bad spirits trapped in the tomb of my body, and Carlos, the grave robber, had set me free.

Lance ran a hand through his hair. "I'm sure it's tough…dealing with it. I can't even imagine. We can get you help, though. I want to help—"

"Lance," I cut in gently. "It's not that either. I don't want to go back. I realized I'd become an agent for the wrong reasons."

His expression fell. "God, Samantha. *Him?* I didn't like him even before…well. Before. And I know you said you had the phone, but I still think he's dirty. I tried opening up an investigation with internal, but they were—"

"You did what?" Panic beat in my chest. Hell, I'd thought everything was clear. I'd thought Ian was safe.

"I tried, but it didn't work. That's what I'm saying. I hit a wall from every angle. Someone from higher up is putting a lid on this entire case. They're shutting it down. It's a cover up."

I felt mildly nauseous. Worry and relief were a volatile mix, combusting in my stomach. "A cover up?"

"Yeah, I mean, at first I thought it might be about you. Covering up that one of their agents got captured." A red stain colored his cheeks. "That was my fault. They should have fired me. Or brought me up on charges."

"Lance," I protested in surprise.

"I was the one who got knocked out, and when I

woke up you were gone. I should have been more careful. I should have *protected* you." He turned away, heaving a breath, and I saw how much this had torn him up.

I put a hand on his arm. "Lance, I don't blame you. This wasn't your fault. You've been a good friend to me."

"I'm sure you thought that when we were in Brody's office," he said bitterly.

"I was pissed," I admitted. "But I know you were doing what you thought was right. Look, it was a shitty situation, but it's over now."

He looked sad and a little lost. "Is it? You're not coming back. Things won't be the same."

No, things could never go back to the way they were. But this was how they needed to be. "I'm sorry," I repeated, ending more than the conversation. Ending a friendship.

He looked at me. He looked away. Quickly, he bent down and kissed my cheek. He murmured in my ear, "Just watch out for yourself, okay? The cover up could have come from Carlos's people. There's still a chance he tipped them off."

Regret swelled inside my chest. God, he was so smart. So caring. And so not for me. On impulse, I kissed his cheek too.

"I'm fine," I promised him. "Better than I've ever been. Now go be an agent. I know you're a great one."

"I did get assigned a case," he said shyly. Then he grumbled, "Would have been more fun with you as my partner. The one I have wants me to pick up his dry cleaning."

I grinned. "Pick up his dry cleaning *and* solve the case."

"Yes, ma'am." His smile fell. "Bye, Samantha."

My throat closed up, and I could only nod in acknowledgement as he got in his car and left.

I sighed, leaning my forehead against the porch pillar. That was rough. He was a nice guy. A good friend. I would have preferred to keep in touch, but that would never do. Not as long as Ian was in my life.

But how long would that be for? We'd joked about private islands, but no promises had been made. I didn't even *know* him.

No, that was a lie. I did know him. I could have dated a guy and seen the clean-cut buttoned-up side of him for five years and still not have known him as well as I knew Ian now. I knew the side of him that kidnapped people, that hurt them. I knew the side that saved lives. I even knew the kicked-back casual side of him, down-to-earth and curiously solicitous in my kitchen. And in every incarnation, I felt the warmth of his attention. That much was constant. That was his love.

CHAPTER NINETEEN

I HAD PROVED, to myself and to Ian, what I really wanted when I turned Lance away on the porch. But in doing so, I had stripped myself down and bared my deepest desires. Not the innocent fairytale I'd always claimed to want, but the shadows beneath it.

My dream wasn't to be a princess in a castle. I wanted to be Persephone, claimed by the god of the underworld. Except that was the thing about getting captured; it wasn't up to me.

I couldn't look at Hennessey as I passed him. I went straight to the shower and turned the knob to scalding.

My head pounded with regret and longing, with betrayal and hope for a future I didn't deserve. Ian didn't deserve it either, so we couldn't even bank on his karmic balance. This white picket house and his dreams of an island were fantasies we spun. Reality was being alone and afraid. Reality was standing underneath a pounding spray of hot water but knowing I'd never really be clean.

The bathroom door opened silently, spilling cool air onto my overheated skin. The shower curtain was a fabric boho confection I'd ordered online, because I sought out everything older than me, everything sweeter and poignant. But even my attempts to be normal were twisted into a parody of romance. Tattered lace and patent leather shoes with red spray across them. I didn't know how to be what society wanted from me. I couldn't change myself, not even for him.

He was naked. I could tell from the warm hair-roughened feel of him—his chest against my back, his arms circling mine. Something firm and hot nudging my ass. His mouth bent to my ear.

"What did Lance have to say?" Ian asked.

I swallowed, feeling sick to my stomach. "He warned me to stay away from you."

"I see. And end up with him instead, I'm guessing. Would you ride off into the sunset together?"

"Maybe," I whispered even though it wasn't true.

"Samantha, love. What makes you think I'd let you leave?"

My eyes fell shut, and the hot tracks down my cheeks didn't come from the shower. I turned in his arms, blindly, gladly. God. All I'd ever wanted was someone to keep me. To want me, even knowing my faults. Like everything I'd ever sought out myself, with peeling paint and uneven edges and a tendency to fall apart. All I'd ever wanted was to be loved.

I sought his mouth with mine and found it. He responded with aching tenderness, his sigh a caress. He gently bit down on my bottom lip, and I whimpered. His tongue laved the spot. That was how it would be between us, the pain and the comfort. The curse of the past and the hope for a future.

He touched me everywhere; he surrounded me. I felt consumed by him, taken within him instead of a separate being. There was no part of me left sacred, no shame he didn't chase away with a tender touch and a pinch of pain. He made every part of me his own—his own thing to have and to hold, to kiss and to hurt—and left no room for the doubt that had chased me my whole life.

Large hands stroked my breasts and tugged my nipples while I squirmed. He held me up, serving himself as he bent his head to lick and kiss and bite the sensitized flesh. I danced on my tiptoes, groaning at the onslaught and holding onto his shoulders to stay afloat.

He ran his fingertips down my belly to the bare skin of my sex.

"God, sweetheart," he said hoarsely. "You're so soft here. So sweet."

And then proceeded to prove his point. He pushed me flush against the wall and knelt before me. I cried out at the cold tile on my back but subsided at the first touch of his lips to my cunt. He crowned the plump outer lips with chaste, tender kisses before nudging my legs apart, before slipping his tongue in the slick space between. His tongue flicked my clit in an age-old rhythm that my body knew by heart.

My hips found the beat and rocked into him in time, seeking release without my consent. My fingers scrabbled at the slippery shower wall behind me, trying to hold me up and failing. I fell in a long, slow slide down the faintly ridged tile wall, held up only by the hot pressure of his mouth and the two fingers he slipped inside me.

He draped one of my legs over his shoulder, and I opened to him. With easier access, he pushed deeper inside me, he assaulted my clit with the lash of his tongue. I couldn't even try to hold myself up like this. I could only wait, wedged between the tile and his body, between a rock and a hard place, and plead wordlessly, with desperate sounds and hungry gasps until I broke. I shattered into pieces with the final clash of him at my core. I splintered and flew in every direction, lost in the mindless pleasure and abject devotion, open and defenseless against the care he was determined to give me, and found myself drenched and boneless on the ceramic floor.

He'd laid me down gently, but now he stood above me. He looked down upon me, and I wanted to revel in his gaze like a night flower beneath the moon. He set his foot on my belly, his toes just beneath my breasts, the slight pressure only a fraction of the force he could inflict. This was payback for the kitchen and so much more as he moved his foot higher. As he curled his toes over my nipple and caught it like a bear trap, pinching me, while I jerked and shuddered on the bathtub floor.

Placing his feet on either side of my head, he straddled my shoulders, looking down. He seemed impossibly fierce this way, dominating me with his cock, slick and heavy. Water sluiced down his shoulders and over his muscled chest. It formed a waterfall around his cock and splashed down onto me, miming the climax still to come. With water. Only clean, fresh water, and what I craved was only what he could give me.

I bent my head to the side so that I could kiss his ankle. I moved to the arch of his foot, praising him with my kisses, worshipping him. I kissed his toes too, while he stared down at me with dark dominion, silently approving. I knew what to do because he'd shown me. Hadn't he taught me? Hadn't he trained me? I knew how he wanted my mouth on his foot because he'd done the same to me. When I had found every inch of skin with my mouth, I switched feet. I curled up on my side, my arms wrapped around his leg, debasing myself and exalting. Kissing his skin and reveling in the pleasure it gave him.

When he'd had enough, he nudged me back to center. I lay on my back and waited for direction. He lowered himself to his knees, so that his cock could press against my lips. I was learning that this was one of his favorite positions. Not just having me suck him, but fucking my face. Kissing my feet and having me worship his. These kinks he blushed to say aloud.

I remembered once thinking how much it said about a man whether he liked to fuck a woman in the pussy or in the ass. Whether he paid extra if she bled. I understood Ian better because of his deviations. I was hungry for them, and the knowledge they could impart. I peeled back each preference like a layer of skin, leaving him vulnerable. He knew how open it left him too. That was why he tied me up, blindfolded and gagged me, just so he could beat me. Artificial shields, but they were gone now.

I wanted him, wholly and without reservation, but somehow I knew he wanted me to resist. Not a fight, just a little reluctance to sharpen the moment. He'd trained me to do all of this, with whips and benches and ball gags. And the reward for learning my lessons was this—his body. His mind. Every part of him with me.

I pressed my lips together to refuse, and he slapped my face. "Take it. Come on, be good, or I'll have to punish you."

Eyes wide with fear and excitement, I shook my head and left my lips together. He slapped me again, and again, until hot tears sprang to my eyes. Until I cried out on impact and cowered beneath him. I thought he would hold my nose to make me open, like he'd done once before. When I'd bitten him. But he did something else, instead. There was more to learn; there always would be. He reached down, full force, and stuck his fingers inside my mouth until I gagged on them. It was undignified and wholly encompassing, so that all I could taste or see or feel was him.

"You'll get better at that," he promised. "For now, though, you'll just have to struggle."

He pushed his cock inside, thick and wet and slippery. With all the water on his body, in my mouth, it felt like I was going to drown, and I gagged, spitting water up against his body. It didn't slow him, didn't matter.

He kept his thumb inside my mouth, deep against the juncture of my jaw, holding it open. His cock invaded me in slow, easy thrusts while I struggled beneath him.

When he came, the salty fluid filled my mouth. It was hard to swallow, struggling like this. For a moment, I panicked, my eyes bulging, body jerking. I was going to drown, not on water, not on his cock, but on his creamy come. In that moment, I had a choice. I could go down fighting or accept my fate. Which was the more dignified answer? I was too panicked to really think it through, but my path had been laid out for me a long time ago. Foretold by events that had led inexorably to this. I closed my eyes and let it wash over me, resigned to my downfall and wishing for it. The muscles in my throat relaxed and I felt them move convulsively, spasming, pulling his deposit down my throat. In a long, desperate rattle, I sucked in a breath, finally clear and unobstructed.

Without being totally lucid, I heard the water turn off. I felt a thick towel enfold me, felt myself lifted and carried. I curled up on my side in the soft refuge of my bed. And when I stirred enough to reach for him, he was there. He comforted me and rocked me to sleep, safe in his arms.

✧　✧　✧

CRIMINALS ALWAYS MADE mistakes.

I'd learned that a long time ago. My job as an agent had been to find those mistakes, to catch them. As Ian

Hennessey said to me once, the nature of detective work was to always be one step behind. FBI agents were hunters—and our prey had a large headstart and very big guns.

As I sat on the couch curled into Ian's side, I couldn't have said which one of us was the hunter and which one of us was prey. I'd been tasked with finding and stopping him at any price. And I had done so. All it had cost was my freedom. Freedom from the shame that had dogged me my whole life. I'd caught him, but he'd caught me right back. This was the trap he'd set, to bind us together so tightly we'd never break free. We'd never want to.

We sat in the dark, bathed by a steady flame of a few candles on the mantel. Dusk had fallen with its usual quickness, arriving fast and late in the summertime. It lent us an air of privacy that I craved right now. What I'd told Ian about living on some secluded island forever and ever was true. I'd go stir crazy without human interaction for years. But right now, I needed time away. To think. To breathe.

To feel safe for the first time since I was a little kid.

Strange that I would feel safer bound and gagged. But I did, because I knew he was looking out for me. He was in charge of me, and all I had to do was rest in his strong embrace.

Supper had been light with fresh tamales from a nearby street vendor, a triangle of Gruyere cheese, and a bunch of plump green grapes. I worried that it wouldn't be hearty enough for Ian's appetite, considering the burger and shake he'd wolfed down at the diner. But he hadn't balked at the meal, and I remembered, too, the more subtle, wholesome dishes he'd served me in captivity. He'd filled his roles, the cultured criminal and jaded agent, so completely that even his dietary preferences were pre-selected—along with his clothes, his mannerisms, and his sexual predilections. It made me sad. It made me want to know the real him.

He showed that to me when dinner was over. He washed the dishes while I dried them, and when the last plate was put away I turned to him, mouth open around a word, caught by the desire in his expression.

"Shh," he murmured. "I love your sweet voice. I want to hear everything you can tell me. But not right now. Now I need a good little whore to use. You can do that for me, can't you?"

He pressed his thumb on my tongue. My eyes widened, my heartbeat raced. But I didn't fight him. Just let him invade my mouth, tasting the faint tang of soap on his skin. I nodded.

He didn't need the coarse ropes or chains to bind me. He found a silky rope tying back the curtains in the kitchen to bind my wrists behind my back. My cheeks heated painfully when he dug through my nightstand and found the purple vibrator that fit inside me perfectly. The dishtowel I'd used to dry the dishes served as a gag, damp and thick on my tongue. Most of my clothes stayed on, but he opened the buttons of my sheer pink blouse and pulled my breasts from the peach-colored camisole. The feather-light ruffles framed my breasts, their color matching my nipples.

As I lay on the couch in his arms, his heart beat steadily beneath my cheek. He stroked my breasts and pinched my nipples with lazy movements, staring into the distance. I would have thought him completely unaffected, except I could feel his thick erection at my hip.

On a particularly cruel twist of my exposed flesh, I whimpered against the damp fabric.

"You like that, don't you, pretty girl."

Not really a question. I wasn't fully a person like this. I was an object for him to use, to see. I was like the vintage milk jug on the mantel with its potted daisies. Something nice to look at. Something to care for.

"No," he continued, "I don't think it will be much of a sacrifice for you at all. I bet you're already wet for me, aren't you? Already drenching that smooth plastic. Getting yourself lubed up like a good girl."

Remote in hand, he flipped on the television. My eyes closed in mortification. God. I wasn't even enough of a distraction for that. He needed more entertainment than me, tied and bared to him. We watched a few minutes of a cooking competition where the chefs put modern twists on ethnic classics. I could have been interested in it if he weren't constantly touching, plucking, smoothing my sensitive skin.

His hands were skilled, knowledgeable, and they brought me to a fever pitch with a few flicks. Not only that, I had to admit. The way he tied me up, the way he used me—that turned me on as well.

He glanced down at his watch and changed the channel again. He didn't check with me to see what I wanted to watch. I wasn't even in the equation. Just a thing, with no preferences, no wishes of my own. It was an old action flick this time. We watched a few minutes while he rolled my nipple between forefinger and thumb.

Slowly, I got the impression he was waiting for something. The clock beside the daisies showed eight seventeen. Not really a time that something typically happened. But then, Ian was far from typical.

When the minute hand moved once…twice…an interruption came over the screen.

Breaking News, it said in block letters across the top of the screen. A pretty reporter spoke seriously into a microphone. Behind her, swarms of people crowded a podium set up beside the courthouse. And at the bottom of the picture, a blue information bar claimed, 'International Criminal Presumed Dead in Aggressive FBI Raid.'

In smaller letters beneath it, it read: *Laguardia has been on the Most Wanted list for 10 years.*

My body jerked in place, unable to move, unable to think. Dead? Of course, he was warm and very much alive beneath me. His hands continued to stroke me but their tenor changed. More calming now.

Soothing.

The woman's voice finally registered, authoritative and clipped. "The alleged drug lord was caught in a massive explosion aboard a steamer just off the Houston Ship Channel after a confrontation with a joint task force involving the FBI, the DEA, and the Coast Guard. Critics are already questioning the lack of due process in regards to the sudden raid, but the FBI spokesperson claims that this is a major win for the Bureau."

The video switched to a row of metal rooftops. Above them, a plume of black smoke suddenly rose up. It hung in the air, a hot air balloon made of soot instead of cloth. The newsreel flipped again to a closer shot of the podium. Brody stood behind the microphones, looking smug, speaking nonsense about impressive planning and foresight.

God. *Foresight.* As if they could look into the future, when they hadn't even seen what was right in front of them.

Lance stood in the background, wearing a suit and appearing very serious. I hoped he got a promotion out of this. At least someone had done been doing his job.

The TV flicked off, leaving only a black screen. I could still see the images on the dark reflective surface.

The anchor woman.

Thick smoke hanging in the air.

FBI agents, smug and misguided.

"I did that for you," Ian murmured in my ear. "That's what I gave up for you. My whole life. My past. But you're going to make up for it, aren't you?"

I whimpered, unsure what he wanted. Unsure what I could take.

I couldn't comprehend the magnitude of what I'd seen on the news. He'd cut off part of himself, just now, with a staged explosion designed to ensure the FBI left us alone. They had no incentive to keep looking, now that they had their closure. Their fucking commendations.

That criminal part of him had been hurting him, decaying. But even though he was better off without it, losing it had to hurt. His pain echoed through my body. His loss became my own.

I expected his anger. I would have preferred it, but his hands were gentle. He turned me so I faced down on the sofa. Implacable and tender, he flipped up my skirt and tugged down my panties. Exposing my ass.

"Yes," he murmured. "You're going to make it all better."

He smacked me on the ass with an open hand, causing more shock than pain. Too soft, really. I deserved worse, and he knew it. I heard the snap of leather as he took off his belt. He pressed my wrists to the base of my back. The first blow was fire across my skin, embers underneath. I screamed into the dishtowel, blow after blow.

I fought him too, but it was too late for that.

When he worked one slippery finger into my ass, then two, I stilled. It was the least I could do, a small penance for the sins I had made. The pillow dried my tears. I was ready for him when he finally mounted me. I breathed through the burn and bore down on him—and let him in deeper. With my pain and my patience, I soothed him, the way he'd done for me. In the process, I soothed myself, because my heart was still pounding after seeing those news reports. After imagining, for a split second, they were true. That he wasn't alive and hurting me. Imagining he had died.

I had to remind myself he was safe. Scratch that. He was *mine*.

I may have been the one with my hands tied behind my back. I may have had thick cock pressed inside my ass, pushing and pushing to the rhythm that he liked. It may have hurt, and fuck, it did, it did. But he was mine. I'd caught him. And I was going to keep him.

CHAPTER TWENTY

I SAW HIS shadow first, a wavery blur from beneath the water. With a kick and a burst of speed, I broke through the surface of the water and breathed deeply. Island air felt sharper. Cleaner, after spending most of my life in the inner city. We had travelled since leaving Houston. Mexico. Argentina. Egypt. Always staying in warm places.

Ian stood on the porch, elbows resting on the porch rail. He wore only loose slung pants made from a linen local to the area. The sun kissed the golden skin of his back, the dappled silver-brown of his hair.

Even from here I could see one eyebrow rise. "What are you wearing?"

I swam to the edge of the pool. "Funny thing. I couldn't find my swimsuit anywhere. You wouldn't know anything about that, would you?"

"I thought we agreed you weren't going to wear that anymore."

He liked to watch me swim naked. I would have simply obeyed him...but sometimes disobeying was more fun. Watching his eyes darken in displeasure. Having him use the offending swimsuit to bind my hands. Knowing he got rid of it after that.

I never did find it. Now I wore a thin tank top instead with thin lace straps. My darker nipples were visible through the wet ribbed fabric. It was a taunt, really. And he knew it.

"Come here."

Flashing him a cowed look, a fake one, I climbed out of the pool. Scratch that. I glided. The gliding part came naturally in the glittering pool with its infinity edge, a steeped plane like a crystal white beach of concrete. The pool was the one nod to overt luxury here. That and the hot tub inside. Otherwise, the house was small and rustic, built with local timber and filled with handcrafted rugs. He'd brought me here for a getaway and I hadn't yet been able to leave. It was too beautiful, too safe. Someday soon we'd travel again, but I always wanted to return here.

Lush foliage blocked us from view. Island security took care of the rest. He hadn't owned a whole island. He owned part of one. He shared it with an ex-Hollywood director and some sort of oil baron from the Middle East, both of whom were more concerned about aerial snapshots being taken than we were.

Royalty. That's how Mia had described his parents' lifestyle. Glittering parties with *la familia*. And though Carlos had money, he'd always preferred things understated. He purchased things he'd never been able to get as a child. Privacy. Safety.

Comfort.

I understood about that. I climbed the cedar porch steps to reach him. He waited for me with hooded eyes, his body taut. Droplets slid down my skin, caressing me. His gaze dipped to my breasts. He wasn't unaffected by me. I could tell by the way his hands clenched. And from the impressive tenting of his pants.

I remembered the grainy black and white photograph from the Bureau. The way he'd stared at the camera. The way he'd stared at me. He looked at me the same way now, in challenge, with wanting.

"Strip, love." His voice was low, guttural.

Flashing him a look beneath my lashes, I reached down and pulled the damp fabric off. My breasts bounced lightly in the sunlight.

"No more swimsuits. No more anything. When you're swimming, I want to see those pretty breasts in the water. I want to see them get tan in the sun. Understand?"

My nipples tightened beneath his hungry gaze, under the lash of his words. I nodded, unable to speak.

"Turn around."

As soon as I faced away, he grabbed me. He maneuvered my body so I faced the pool, and he put my hands on the railing. *Hold on,* he told me with a squeeze of my wrists. He kicked my legs apart while his broad hands pulled my hips up. In seconds, I was positioned for him. So ready for him.

He might have spanked me then, in pretend punishment for my transgressions, but he was further gone than I realized. The blunt head of his cock nudging me was my only warning. Then he thrust inside, to the hilt, a sudden stretch that had me on my tiptoes, crying out.

His growl filled the air and vibrated his chest behind me. "Does it hurt? It's your fault for being that way. So beautiful I have to take you." He slapped the soft underside of my ass, and I clenched around him. "And so fucking tight."

He pulled back and pushed back in, so hard and fast I felt invaded. I ached with him, so full and so tender. He told me how he felt with every punishing thrust, how angry he was and how dark. How hard it was to love to me, but he did it anyway. He couldn't have helped it. We were trapped together in these bonds of our own making.

With a rough pull, he tilted my hips up. His cock hit a certain point inside that made me moan. My mouth opened around the sound, helpless and hungry. I could do nothing in this position except take it. I could only wait for him to speed up, to move inside me faster and harder, to reach around and pinch my clit so I came around him, wet and hot.

His body stiffened. His hands tightened on my hips. A rough, guttural sound rumbled behind me as he came. His cock pulsed against my walls, and my sex tightened around him in response. We communed that way, while he rocked through the last of his climax.

The slow slide of his cock pulling out was enough to make me whimper. He turned me around and pushed me onto the deck. On my knees, I knew what to do. He'd trained me well. I leaned forward and mouthed his half-erect cock, licking it clean.

"How do you taste, love? Sweet, aren't you?"

I closed my eyes as a flush heated my cheeks. He still knew how to embarrass me, and he wielded that knowledge like a weapon. I was forever slayed around him, bleeding and raw. I wouldn't have thought it possible just six months ago, when I'd been wrapped up in so many layers. He'd carefully ripped down each one.

I licked every trace of our come from his cock and regretfully covered him up. With gentle hands, he gathered my wet hair and used it as a leash to guide me into the shade. He sat down in the rough Adirondack chair while I knelt on the plush cushion in front of him. I rested my cheek against his knee, curled up at his feet.

His dark gaze warmed me, because I knew I'd returned his gift of peace. Other people wouldn't understand. They'd only see the control he used with me, the violence he wreaked. But that was only the outside, the drawbridge and cannons of a fortress heavily guarded. I'd been inside. I knew the truth.

He took me roughly because it was the only way he could. He spoke to me cruelly because he knew I liked it best. And he held my hips so tightly, he left those finger-shaped bruises on my skin, because he couldn't bear to let me go.

THE END

THANK YOU!

Thank you for reading Don't Let Go! I hope you enjoyed Carlos and Samantha's story…

- Keep reading with my dark romance Wanderlust.

- Would you like to know when my next book is released? You can sign up for my newsletter at skyewarren.com/newsletter.

- Like me on Facebook at facebook.com/skyewarren.

- I appreciate your help in spreading the word, including telling a friend.

- Reviews help readers find books! Leave a review on your favorite book site.

- Turn the page for an excerpt from Wanderlust…

WANDERLUST

Evie always dreamed of seeing the world, but her first night at a motel turns into a nightmare. Hunter is a rugged trucker willing to do anything to keep her—including kidnapping. As they cross the country in his rig, Evie plots her escape, but she may find what she's been looking for right beside her.

> *"Brace yourself for an unlikely and intense love story. There are no heroes in this tale, only disturbingly beautiful monsters."*
>
> —Romantic Book Affairs

Excerpt from Wanderlust

I FELT TINY out here. Would it always be this way now that I was free? Our seclusion at home had provided more than security. An inflated sense of pride, diminishing the grand scheme of things to raise our own importance. On this deserted sidewalk in the middle of nowhere, it was clear how very insignificant I was. No one even knew I was here. No one would care.

When I rounded the corner, I saw that the lights in the gas station were off. Frowning, I tried the door, but it was locked. It seemed surreal for a moment, as if maybe it had never been open at all, as if this were all a dream.

Unease trickled through me, but then I turned and caught site of the sunset. It glowed in a symphony of colors, the purples and oranges and blues all blending together in a gorgeous tableau. There was no beauty like this in the small but smoggy city where I had come from, the skyline barely visible from the tree in our backyard. This sky didn't even look real, so vibrant, almost blinding, as if I had lived my whole life in black and white and suddenly found color.

I put my hand to my forehead, just staring in awe.

My God, was this what I'd been missing? What else

was out there, unimagined?

I considered going back for my camera but for once I didn't want to capture this on film. Part of my dependence on photography had been because I never knew when I'd get to see something again, didn't know when I'd get to go outside again. I was a miser with each image, carefully secreting them into my digital pockets. But now I had forever in the outside world. I could breathe in the colors, practically smell the vibrancy in the air.

A sort of exuberant laugh escaped me, relief and excitement at once. Feeling joyful, I glanced toward the neat row of semi-trucks to the side. Their engines were silent, the night air still. The only disturbance: a man leaned against the side of one, the wispy white smoke from his cigarette curling upward. His face was shrouded in darkness.

My smile faded. I couldn't see his expression, but some warning bell inside me set off. I sensed his alertness despite the casual stance of his body. His gaze felt hot on my skin. While I'd been watching the sunset, he'd been watching me.

When he suddenly straightened, I tensed. Where a second ago I'd felt free, now my mother's warnings came rushing back, overwhelming me. Would he come for me? Hurt me, attack me? It would only take a few minutes to run back to my room—could I beat him there? But all he did was raise his hand, waving me around the side of the building. I circled hesitantly and found another entrance, this one to a diner.

Hesitantly, I waved my thanks. After a moment, he nodded back.

"Paranoid," I chastised myself.

The diner was wrapped with metal, a retro look that was probably original. Uneven metal shutters shaded the green windows, where an OPEN sign flickered.

Inside, turquoise booths and brown tables lined the walls. A waitress behind the counter looked up from her magazine. Her hair was a dirty blonde, darker than mine, pulled into a knot. A thick layer of caked powder and red lipstick were still in place, but her eyes were bloodshot, tired.

"I heard we got a boarder," she said, nodding to me. "First one of the year."

I blinked. It was a cool April night. If I was the first one of the year, then that was a long time to go without boarders.

"What about all the trucks outside?"

"Oh, they sleep in their cabs. Those fancy new leather seats are probably more comfortable than those old mattresses filled with God-knows-what." She laughed at her own joke, revealing a straight line of grayish teeth.

I managed a brittle smile then ducked into one of the booths.

She sidled over with a notepad and pen.

"We don't usually see girls as pretty as you around here. Especially alone. You don't got nobody to look after you?"

The words were spoken in accusation, turning a compliment into a warning.

"Just passing through," I said.

She snorted. "Aren't we all? Okay, darlin', what'll it be?"

Under her flat gaze, I turned the sticky pages of the menu, ignoring the stale smells that wafted up from it. Somehow the breakfast food seemed safest. I hoped it would be easier to avoid food poisoning with pancakes than a steak.

After the waitress took my order, I waited, tapping my fingers on the vinyl tabletop to an erratic beat. I was a little nervous—jittery, although there was no reason to be. Everyone had been nice. Not exactly welcoming, but then I was a stranger. Had I expected to make friends with the first people I met?

Yes, I admitted to myself, somewhat sheepishly. I had rejected my mother's view that everyone was out to get me, but neither was everyone out to help me. I would do well to retain some of the wariness she'd instilled in me. A remote truck stop wasn't the place to meet people, to make lasting relationships. That would be later, once I had started my job. No, even later than that, when I'd saved up enough to reach Niagara Falls. Then I could relax.

When my food came, I savored the sickly sweet syrup that saturated my pancakes. It would rot my teeth, my mother would have said. Well, she wasn't here. A small rebellion, but satisfying and delicious.

The bell over the door rang, and I glanced up to see a man come in. His tan T-shirt hung loose while jeans hugged his long legs. He was large, strong—and otherwise unremarkable. He might have come from any one of those eighteen-wheelers out there, but somehow I knew he'd been the one watching me.

His face had been in the shadows then, but now I could see he had a square jaw darkened with stubble and lips quirked up at the side. Even those strong features paled against the bright intensity of his eyes, both tragic and terrifying. So brown and deep that I could fall into them. The scary part was the way he stared—insolently. Possessively, as if he had a right to look at me, straight in my eyes and down my neckline to peruse my body.

I suddenly felt uncomfortable in this dress, as if it exposed too much. I wished I hadn't changed clothes. More disturbing, I wished I had listened to my mother. I looked back down at my pancakes, but my stomach felt stretched full, clenched tight around the sticky mass I'd already eaten.

I wanted to get up and leave, but the waitress wasn't here and I had to pay the bill. More than that, it would be silly to run away just because a man looked at me. That was exactly what my mom would do.

Back when we still left the house, someone would just glance at her sideways in the grocery store. Then we'd flee to the car where she'd do breathing exercises before she could drive us home. I was trying to escape that. I *had* escaped that. I wouldn't go back now just because a man with pretty eyes checked me out.

Still, it was unnerving. When I peeked at him from beneath my lashes, I met his steady gaze. He'd seated himself so he had a direct line of vision to me. Shouldn't he be more circumspect? But then, I wouldn't know what was normal. I was clueless when it came to public interaction. So I bowed my head and poked at the soggy pancakes.

Once the waitress gave me the bill, I'd leave. Simple enough. Easy, for someone who wasn't paranoid or crazy. And I wasn't—that was my mother, not me. I could do this.

When the waitress came out, she went straight to his table. I drew little circles in the brown syrup just to keep my eyes off them. I couldn't hear their conversation, but I assumed he was ordering his meal.

Finally, the waitress approached my table, wearing a more reserved expression than she had before. Almost cautious. I didn't fully understand it, but I felt a flutter of nerves in my full stomach.

She paused as if thinking of the right words. Or maybe wishing she didn't have to say them. "The man over there has paid for your meal. He'd like to join you."

I blinked, not really understanding. The gentleness of her voice unnerved me. More than guilt—pity.

"I'm sorry." I fumbled with the words. "I've already eaten. I'm done."

"You have food left on your plate. Doesn't matter how much you want to eat anyway." She paused and then carefully strung each word along the sentence. "He requests the pleasure of your company."

My heart sped up, the first stirrings of fear.

I supposed I should feel flattered, and I did in a way. He was a handsome man, and he'd noticed me. Of course, I was the only woman around besides the waitress, so it wasn't a huge accomplishment. But I wasn't prepared for fielding this kind of request. Was this a common thing, to pay for another woman's meal?

It was a given that I should say no. Whatever he wanted from me, I couldn't give him, so it was only a question of letting him down nicely.

"Please tell him thank you for the offer. I appreciate it, I do. But you see, I really am finished with my meal and pretty tired, so I'm afraid it won't be possible for him to join me. Or to pay for my meal. In fact, I'd like the check, please."

Her lips firmed. Little lines appeared between her brows, and with a sinking feeling I recognized something else: fear.

"Look, I know you aren't from around here, but that there is Hunter Bryant." When I didn't react to the name, her frown deepened. "Here's a little advice from one woman to another. There are some men you just don't say no to. Didn't your mama ever warn you about men like that?"

Want to read more? Wanderlust at Amazon.com, BarnesAndNoble.com, and iBooks..

OTHER BOOKS BY SKYE WARREN

Wanderlust

On the Way Home

Hear Me

Prisoner

Dark Nights Series

Keep Me Safe (prequel)

Trust in Me

Don't Let Go

The Beauty Series

Beauty Touched the Beast

Beneath the Beauty

Broken Beauty

Beauty Becomes You

The Beauty Series Compilation

Standalone Erotic Romance

His for Christmas

Take the Heat: A Criminal Romance Anthology

Sweetest Mistress

Below the Belt

Dystopia Series

Leashed

Caged

About The Author

Skye Warren is the New York Times and USA Today Bestselling author of dark romance. Her books are raw, sexual and perversely romantic.

Sign up for Skye's newsletter:
www.skyewarren.com/newsletter

Like Skye Warren on Facebook:
facebook.com/skyewarren

Follow Skye Warren on Twitter:
twitter.com/skye_warren

Visit Skye's website for her current booklist:
www.skyewarren.com

COPYRIGHT

This is a work of fiction. Any resemblance to actual persons, living or dead, business establishments, events or locales is entirely coincidental. All rights reserved. Except for use in a review, the reproduction or use of this work in any part is forbidden without the express written permission of the author.

Don't Let Go © 2013 by Skye Warren
Print Edition

Cover design by Book Beautiful
Formatting by BB eBooks
Edited by Madison Seidler

ISBN: 9781492996002

13223714R00168

Made in the USA
Lexington, KY
28 October 2018